FOREVER DECEMBER

GODS OF CHAOS MOTORCYCLE CLUB

HONEY PALOMINO

PROLOGUE

"*C*an you keep a secret?"

I didn't know it at the time, but those few words, carelessly strewn together and spontaneously blurted out, would prove to be the very words that would change my life forever.

"Of course," I replied, thinking that I'd already been keeping my own secret for a few years now, so of course I could keep December's too.

December was my best friend's sister. I happened to be in love with her, but that was my secret. There were times when I was sure she knew, like when she looked at me with that slow side glance after I'd laughed at one of her jokes or something.

But I never told her.

We kissed once — on a cold, snowy night that seems like it was a million years ago and yesterday, all at once. If I close my eyes, I can still feel her lips on mine and the snowflakes falling on my eyelids.

After Leo, her brother and my best friend, found out a few days later, it was like I'd opened the gates of hell. He was furious. So, reluctantly, I backed off.

He was my best friend, after all.

But my feelings for December only intensified over the years, morphing into a full blown, silent obsession, if I'm being honest. And while it may have been a quiet, secret obsession, it raged inside of me like a hot flame I couldn't seem to extinguish.

December moved on, though, much to my dismay.

Her boyfriend, Shane, was also friends with Leo, but for some reason Leo didn't object to her dating him as much as he did me kissing her once.

I don't know why.

To put it bluntly, Shane was a dick. Everyone knew it.

No matter how hard I tried, I couldn't figure out what December saw in him. In the end, I figured it was because he was older than us, if only by a few years.

Despite my unending crush on her, I kept my opinions about Shane and the entire situation to myself. My friends were all I had, and the four of us created a little tribe that I valued way too much to risk by opening my mouth, no matter how much I thought December deserved better.

So, I tried to be a good friend to December and let that be enough for me.

But it was never enough.

The fact that she wanted to share a secret with me thrilled me immensely. So, as we sat outside the Grab n-Go in Shane's old beat up Honda, on a hot summer night, waiting for Shane and Leo to grab snacks, and — if they could pull it off, since we were all underage — a little beer for later, and she turned those dark, soulful eyes on me and made me swear on my Mama's grave that I wouldn't tell a soul, I jumped on the chance to prove my loyalty.

It was December's and Leo's eighteenth birthday — the nineteenth of June — and we we're all going to the coast later that night to celebrate. I'd be turning eighteen next month, and Shane was older than all of us, but just by a couple of years.

Just in case they couldn't get the beer, I'd snuck a bottle of whiskey out of my old man's liquor cabinet and hid it in my backpack to present to her later. She was always a little less reserved and the pain that seemed to take up residence in her eyes lately disappeared just a little when we were dancing around the fire with a good buzz.

I'd have done anything to make her happy.

It was going to be a good night and as soon as Shane and Leo got back, we'd be on our way. The sun was already setting, a golden orange glow that held the promise of a new chapter for all of us. Now that we'd all finally graduated, we felt like the world was opening up for us. Like anything could happen.

If we could just get out of Depoe Bay first.

I had no idea at the time just how right I was about that.

"Are you going to tell me now or are you going to wait till they get back?" I laughed, as she hesitated. Her eyes darted past me, looking over my shoulder to check for the guys. She took a deep breath, meeting my gaze again, as if mustering her courage. Hesitating, she bit her bottom lip and I couldn't help but smile. This must be a big secret, because she only did that when she was thinking hard about something.

"I'm pregnant, Wolfe."

Like a dagger to my heart, her words pierced my soul so sharply, that I gasped, not in shock, but in physical pain. I shook my head, hoping the expression on my face didn't reveal my devastation.

"Wow," I whispered. "It's Shane's?"

She looked like I'd slapped her. "Of course, who else's would it be?"

"Right," I nodded, quickly.

The four of us were a tribe, like I said. We didn't really hang out with anyone else. Not that there were that many cool people our age to hang out with anyway. Anyone with half a brain moved away from this tiny coastal town as fast as they could. There were only a thousand residents anyway and it seemed that this summer we were the only ones still hanging around, out of either an obligation to elderly parents — like Leo's and December's folks — or the lack of anywhere else to go — like me and Shane. I wasn't too connected to my dad. Since Mom died of cancer when I was just a kid, Dad had pretty much checked out anyway.

I spent most of my time dreaming about my next move.

3

I was thinking of law school eventually. I knew it would take a lot of work, which was daunting, but the idea excited me. Who was to say I couldn't do it? I was smart and determined. I was tired of being held down by the low expectations of the people in this town. I had a plan, but I didn't have money, so my plan would be accomplished one small step at a time.

"That's wild, December," I finally said, once I saw through my crushed emotions that her face was quickly falling. "What are you going to do?"

"I'm going to keep it, Wolfe." Her voice was quiet and determined and I could tell it was taking all her strength to stay brave. It dawned on me that she was probably terrified.

"What did Shane say?"

"He doesn't know yet. You're the first person I've told," she admitted.

"Me?" I asked, biting my tongue before I asked why. I knew why. I was the only person she really trusted. I may have been devastated at her news, which clearly knocked me out of the running for anything ever happening between us, but I was also proud of the fact that she felt so safe with me. At least it was something.

"I'm going to tell him soon. I just couldn't tell him yet. I don't know why," she said, staring out the window, her eyes stormy and dark. I longed to pull her in my arms and hold her close, tell her everything was going to be okay, no matter what happened, no matter what Shane said.

"Leo's gonna freak out." Her voice was a quiet wisp in the air.

"Maybe," I agreed. He would definitely freak out, I knew that for sure. There wasn't much in this world that Leo loved more than his twin sister. They had loving parents, but they were in their fifties when they adopted the two of them and now that they were in their seventies, Leo and December were mostly responsible for looking out for each other. Leo took his job seriously. "He loves you, though. He might be upset at first, but give him some time. It'll be okay."

"I hope you're right," she said, staring thoughtfully into my eyes.

"I am," I assured her. It was all I could do. She was in the front seat, so hugging her from my spot in the backseat would have been extremely awkward. I reached up and patted her hand, the feel of her skin on mine doing what it always did. I shifted in my seat, pulling my hand back.

Pregnant.

My mind was reeling, trying frantically to rewrite the story I'd imagined for our future. A kid changed everything. Everything.

It was almost too much to even imagine. We'd all gone through a lot, but hell, we were all still kids ourselves. Even Shane was one of the most immature dudes I knew. In fact, it was Shane I was worried about more than anyone. Most likely he would not be taking the news of his imminent fatherhood very well.

He was never the most stable guy in the first place. He had a quick temper and a big ego, both of which weren't the most pleasant traits to have. Shane's family lived hard — his parents and brothers were both drug dealers and his sister was addicted to meth. He spent as much time away from them as he could. Which is why he hung out with us so often, I figured. We liked to party, a little booze, but that was it. And Leo, December, and myself, we were good people. We were fun and easy going and we liked each other — a lot, obviously.

We knew Shane didn't have it so great at home. So, we let him into our circle. And then one thing led to another and he and December hooked up and now…well, there we were sitting in his car and as I absorbed this news, I felt terrible for December.

Did she really know what she was getting into?

I knew there were options, but I also knew she knew about them just as well as I did, and she didn't need me lecturing her or even bringing that up. She'd make up her own mind. It was her body. It was her life.

And she was an adult now, after all. Maybe it wasn't so bad. I knew it would be hard for her, but I had no doubt she'd be an amazing mother.

"Wow, a baby at eighteen," I said.

"It's so cliché, huh?"

I shrugged, smiling at her, "Fuck it."

5

"You're a good friend, Wolfe," she said, her eyes staring into mine and seeming to penetrate straight into my heart. "I love you, dude."

"Forever?" I asked, reciting my usual line.

"Forever." She nodded firmly.

I swallowed hard, "I love you, too."

"Forever?" she asked, a wistful smile stretching across her face. I reached up and grabbed her hand, squeezing it gently.

"Forever," I promised, with all my heart.

It wasn't the first time we'd said it to each other. We all said it. Three little words, freely thrown around like a casual declaration of friendship.

Deep down, my words meant so much more, though. When I said 'forever', I wasn't sure if it meant the same thing as when she said it.

It didn't matter, though. The truth was the truth, and nothing in the world could change my love for her. A wild thought flashed in my mind and I fought with the words attempting to escape my lips. Would she want to hear them? I wanted to tell her I would be there for her and the baby, in case Shane bailed. I wanted her to know she wasn't alone. That she never would be. That she had options. She didn't have to raise this baby with Shane, not if she didn't want to.

It all seemed so important to say and yet so very inappropriate in the moment. She'd not even told him yet. Maybe he would surprise all of us and this would sober him up a little, make him grow up for once.

After a moment, I decided that it could wait. The one thing we all seemed to have right now was time. In fact, time seemed to stretch out before us like a never ending road.

That night felt like the beginning of everything. As if nothing of any real importance had come before it. December wasn't going anywhere, and neither was I. If the right moment came along, then of course, I'd tell her. In the meantime, I'd do what I'd always done — just be a good friend to her.

The driver's side door flew open, violently jarring us out of our quiet moment. Our heads snapped to the side as Shane flung himself behind the wheel, the overhead light of the Honda illuminating the interior of the car.

He was shaking, wild-eyed, and covered in blood.

His white t-shirt was drenched in splattered crimson, with streaks smeared on his neck and cheek.

The next few seconds passed in a blur that I played out in my head a million times afterwards, examining every second with forensic detail.

"Shane, what the fuck?" I demanded, my heart jumping into my throat. I looked out the window, scanning the parking lot. "Where's Leo?"

"He's gone, man," he cried, his voice full of panic. "That fucker! He shot him!"

"What!" I shouted. December screamed. My head snapped over to her at the sound of her anguished cry and I saw that she was huddled back up against the door, attempting to get as far away from Shane as possible, her arms wrapped around her torso.

I'd never seen anyone look like that before and I felt her pain in every ounce of my soul. Time seemed to slow down to a crawl as my eyes scanned her face.

The sound of the engine roaring to life shook me out of my trance.

When Shane put the car in gear, I freaked out.

"What are you doing?" I shouted, my voice booming through the car. He turned his head, his eyes crashing into mine.

I saw nothing but fear.

"We have to fucking get out of here! The cops are coming!"

"Dude, what happened?" I demanded. "Tell me now!"

"Look, man, I was just trying to get some cash."

"I don't understand, you were getting beer...what happened to Leo?"

I tried to slow my mind, but all I could think about was Leo. Shane shook his head and repeated himself. "We gotta go. The cops are gonna be here in a minute, dude."

"I'm not leaving him!" I roared, my voice rising in anger.

Denial washed over me as I took a last glance at December, my hand reaching for the door handle at the same time. I shook my head, and opened the door, my feet hitting the pavement at a dead run.

CHAPTER 1

 HE LETTERS

Wolfe,

Hey.

I can't believe it's been a year. When I saw you at your sentencing hearing, I wanted to crawl across that barrier and hug you so hard. I cried the whole time, I'm pretty sure you heard me. The entire court room probably heard me.

I owe you so much, Wolfe. I don't know how I'll ever repay you. I don't have anything, as you well know. God, I don't even have my brother anymore. Sometimes, it doesn't seem real. And yet, at other times, it's so real it's like a knife that's buried deep and I can't get it out of my heart. That's how it feels most days. I guess the other feeling is really just numbness.

I wonder if you ever feel like that?

I wonder how you are all the time. I think about you all the time. When I'm not thinking about the baby, I guess.

He's so cute, Wolfe. You'd love him. He just started smiling. He tries to hold his head up, but he can't do it for very long and it just wobbles. It's kind of funny. I wish you could see it. It makes the pain of childbirth all worth it. I wish you could have been there. Shane said he couldn't handle all the blood and stuff, so he waited down the street at the bar until it was all over.

I named him Leo. So, now there's another Leo in the family.

Shane keeps calling him Bud, which kind of bugs me, but that's okay.

I'm going to send a picture of us with this letter.

Man, having a baby is so hard. I always heard people say that, but I guess you don't really know how hard something is until you do it. It's exhausting. I hardly ever sleep.

Look at me, complaining. I'm sorry. I shouldn't complain, not to you, of all people.

I can't imagine how hard it must be for you to be in there. I wish I could turn the clock back to that night and insist we never stopped at that station.

I miss Leo so much, Wolfe.

I miss you, too.

Let me know what you think of the picture, okay? I can't wait to hear from you.

Forever,

December

* * *

DECEMBER,

Hey, girl. It was so good to get your letter and the picture of the two of you. You're right, he's adorable. He looks just like you. He has your eyes. And you look great, too. Did you cut your hair? I like it.

I think Leo would be proud of your son, December.

I did hear you crying at the hearing. I hated it. I'm sorry you were so upset. I'm so sorry this is all so hard. I wish I could make it all go away, too. In the moment, it just seemed like the right thing to do. It still does, to be honest. If I had to do it over again, I'd do the exact same thing.

Prison is a completely different world. I guess I'll get used to it. Everyone in here is so hard, and that is probably the most difficult part of it all. I have a good cellmate, though, so that's a good thing. His name is Spike, but I don't really want to know why, so I haven't asked yet. He's been in here a long time already, so he's showing me the ropes. He sleeps a lot, but there's not much else to do, other than work out and go to our jobs. We both work in the kitchen. Mainly, I spend my nighttime hours reading. There's nothing like a good book to help me escape my reality for a few hours. It's the coming back down that gets me. The bars are a constant reminder of where I am and why, and so it's hard to forget for any real length of time. Spike says that's why he sleeps so much. His dreams are his escape.

We have a tiny window and sometimes, I can see the moon hanging over the barbed wire in the distance. I stare at it and wonder if it looks the same where you are. It probably does. I'm not that far away.

Overall, it's not as bad as I imagined. Of course, I had plenty of time to imagine the worst while I was in Juvie waiting for my sentencing, so I guess I'm beginning to breathe a little easier now that I see it's not a constant violent riot, which is what I was imagining. I guess I got lucky, only getting fifteen years. My lawyers said it was because I hadn't turned eighteen yet and I didn't have any priors. It's weird being in an adult prison now. But I guess I'm an adult now. We both are, huh?

December, I want you to move on with your life. Raise your boy, be a good mama to him, and be good to yourself. Don't spend all your time thinking about me. I'm alright. I made this decision. I want to say you don't owe me anything, but you do - you owe it to me to give the both of you a good life, okay? You're the reason I'm here, but not in a bad way. Leo would have wanted it this way. He would have wanted your son to have both of his parents in his life.

Just do that, and all of this will be worth it.

I miss you, too, don't ever think I don't.

Someday this will all be over.

It's only time, right?

Forever,

Wolfe

* * *

11

WOLFE,

It was so nice to hear from you. Sorry it took me a minute to write back. Being a mother is time consuming, and some days, I don't even have time to take a shower. My life consists of breastfeeding and changing diapers and spending hours trying to get Leo to nap. I'm not complaining, though. I realize more every day just how blessed I am.

You probably don't want me to spend a lot of time talking about 'what happened', so I won't. But I just want to say thank you. I'll be in gratitude to you for the rest of our lives. And I promise I'll make sure that Leo knows who you are and what a wonderful man you are. And I promise that what you did won't be in vain. I'll make sure Leo has a great life, Wolfe, and I'll be a good mama, just like you asked.

I got a letter from the prison that I'm approved to visit you now. I'm going to try to come down next month, if our car will make it. Shane's been using it to deliver pizzas lately, so it's getting a lot of use. I'll bring Leo, I can't wait for you to meet him. Who else is on your visitors list? Do you need me to bring anything or mail you anything? Shane doesn't make much money, and I can't get a job yet because hiring a babysitter is so expensive, so I've just been staying home and taking care of him. My parents help a little, but to be honest, their health is failing. Leo's death was so hard on both of them. I'm afraid they won't be around much longer. I'm taking care of them and Leo now, which doesn't leave me any free time at all.

Oh my god, look at me complaining again.

I'm sorry, Wolfe.

Tell me more about what you are doing. I wonder what your schedule is like, how you spend your days. Your cellmate sounds...interesting. I've come up with all kinds of scenarios in my head about how he got his name. If you ever find out, let me know. It'd be nice to know if I'm right.

The baby just started crying. It's the middle of the night, and I couldn't sleep, if you can imagine that, so I wanted to take a few minutes to write you while I had some time alone. I have to go get him now before he wakes up Shane.

Write me back soon, okay?

Forever,

December

* * *

DECEMBER,

Sounds like you have your hands full. I'm so sorry to hear about your parents not doing well. I guess Leo's death impacted us all deeply. He was such a good man. I think about him all the time. I wish I could talk to him. Well, I do, actually. He just doesn't talk back. At least not yet. Wouldn't that be nice, though?

Do you believe in ghosts?

I don't know that I do. I mean, if Leo could come back as a ghost, he probably would have done that by now, I think? I don't know. Maybe there's like a processing time before you can come back or something. Who knows? Well, I guess Leo knows now. He knows the secret about what happens after you die, you know? I'm kind of jealous about that.

December, I know you're busy and don't have a lot of time or money. Don't worry about coming to visit. The drive is over two hours, one way. And that's not easy with a baby, I know that. To be perfectly honest, I don't want you to see me this way. I guess orange isn't my color. And these jumpsuits do nothing for my curves! haha

I'm trying to keep my sense of humor in here. And I keep reminding myself that I got fifteen years, but there's a possibility it could be reduced to ten if I keep my nose clean and stay out of trouble. So far, so good, on that front.

So, what I'm trying to say is that maybe it's best if you don't visit. As much as I'd love to see you, it'll be too hard on you (and the car). I'm glad to hear Shane is working. I hope he's being good to you. Is he a good dad?

Oh! Spike finally told me how he got his nickname. I guess when he was a kid, he had a multi-colored, pointy mohawk and his friends started calling him Spike. Kind of wholesome, compared to the things I was imagining. You'll have to tell me if you imagined that one. He's a good guy, though. I like him. He's a little weird, but who isn't in this place?

I've started taking a few college courses in here. Just some basic stuff, but

I like it. It's nice having something else to think about, something other than the past, or that night, or Leo.

I miss him every single day.

Miss you, too.

Forever,

Wolfe

* * *

WOLFE,

Hey there! Guess what? Leo's getting his first tooth! I'm sending you another picture of him. He can smile and laugh now and he talks — well not words, but he makes all these sounds and he tries to talk so hard, but it's just babbling.

We got a puppy. Well, Shane just brought her home one day out of the blue, actually. He found her outside of the bar he started working at. Remember Peter's Pub? That's where he's working.

I was so mad at first, about the dog, because I was thinking it was just one more thing for me to take care of. But Leo loves her so much, it was hard to stay mad. She's a little black lab, with eyes as dark as the night sky. She chews everything, which is annoying. And she pees everywhere, but I'm trying hard to train her to go outside. Now that it's winter, it's not so fun to have to jump out of bed early every morning to take her out into the cold, but it's better than stepping into a puddle of warm pee when you wake up! So gross! I've contemplated putting a diaper on her — hey, it works for Leo!

Thanks for sharing the origin of Spike's name. No, that was not one of my guesses. I guessed more sinister reasons, just like you did. We always did think alike, didn't we?

I understand you don't want me to visit, but I promise I'll get there someday. And besides, I like the color orange and I bet you look great in it!

Okay, gotta run.

Write back soon!

Forever,

December

* * *

DECEMBER,

A puppy! How fun! What's her name? I'd love to see a picture of her.

I can't believe how big Leo is getting. He's growing so fast. Teeth, already? That's gotta be so cool to watch. I hope he's not in a lot of pain.

I wish they would let us wear another color. You might like orange but I'll never see that color again in the same way as long as I live. No matter where you look in here, it's like a sea of orange. There are so many prisoners. Thousands.

Sometimes, I sit in the yard and stare out at all of them and it's just painful, you know? So many lives wasted. Most just because of a single bad decision. I think about the potential lost, how much good they could have done in their communities. Maybe one of them would have gone on to create a cure for cancer or AIDS or invent something cool, you know? A lot of them are like me. So young. And even with their entire lives stretching out before them, their futures are so bleak. It can be really depressing.

I've learned the key to staying sane in here is to keep your mind busy. I'm really enjoying my classes. I'm taking a creative writing class and a basic math class. After these are done, I'm going to take a history course. Have you thought about going to college, December? You could probably get some loans or grants or something to help pay for classes and books. I mean, it sounds like you're happy being a mom and I know you're so busy right now, but maybe later you might want something for yourself, right? And it would be good to have something to fall back on, you know, just in case.

I forgot to answer your question before, but no, I don't have anyone else on my visitors list. Well, my old man, but after I confessed to the cops to killing the clerk at the store, he basically disowned me. I don't expect I'll be seeing him anytime soon. So, it's just you. I know I said I didn't want you to go out of your way to come see me, but if you do ever find yourself near Salem for whatever reason, then it would be okay if you came by. I think you have to schedule it, so plan ahead, and you better let me know! Don't just spring it on me. I'll need to make sure I comb my hair or something first.

Time keeps flying by and I'm thankful for that.

15

Someday, we'll be able to hang out and there won't be a scrap of orange fabric anywhere in sight!

Forever,

Wolfe

* * *

WOLFE,

I can't believe I haven't written to you in so long. I am so sorry. How are you doing?

Can you believe it? Leo's almost two already! We're doing okay. Things can get rocky sometimes around here. Having a kid wears on you after a while, I guess. Shane and I aren't really getting along so well these days. He's not home much, and that's what we fight about the most, I guess. And money. Always money.

Lately, he's been hanging out with some cops that he met at the bar. I guess there's some training program they're trying to get him to sign up for. So, maybe he'll be a cop someday, too. That seems weird, doesn't it? But I guess it'll bring in more money, so I suppose it's a good thing, no matter how weird.

How are your classes going? What do you write about in your creative writing class? Are you still taking it? I have thought about taking some classes, too, especially after I heard from you last. I just don't know when or how I'd make that happen.

My parents are getting worse. Mom was in the hospital last week, because she fell and broke her hip. I can't believe they sent her home with my dad, like he's supposed to take care of her now. He's too frail to take care of himself.

Leo and Lucy — that's our dog — and I have been staying over there a lot to help out until Mom is back on her feet. Mainly, I cook and clean for them and Leo crashes out on my chest while I sleep on the couch. It doesn't really matter where we sleep, because most nights Shane doesn't come home till morning anyway.

Leo's crying again, I gotta go.

I hope you're doing okay, Wolfe. Take care of yourself.

Forever,

December

* * *

DECEMBER,

Hey, girl.

It was nice to hear from you.

I'm really sorry to hear about your parents, that all sounds so rough. I hope your mom heals up real fast.

I'll be honest, the thought of Shane being a cop is not just weird, it's kind of scary. But if it takes some of the burden off you, then I guess that's a good thing. Trying real hard to wrap my head around that one. Like everything else, I suppose it'll just take time.

Speaking of time, I have to keep this short. I got your letter this morning and I wanted to write you back real quick before I start my day.

When I used to think about what guys did in prison before I got here, I never imagined they would be so busy all the time. The only free time you have is late at night and then it's lights out pretty early and it's hard to get anything done then. I have to squeeze all my reading and studying in before nine every night and with all the work they force you to do in here, it's not easy to do that.

So far, I'm balancing it, but it's a struggle most days.

I'm just trying to keep my nose clean, so I don't get any more time added onto my sentence. I've seen that happen to several of the guys in here and the thought of it is just devastating. Just for getting into a fight, usually.

Anyway, I can't be late.

I hope you're taking care of yourself while you're taking care of everyone else, December.

Forever,

Wolfe

* * *

WOLFE,

I'm coming to visit you!

17

Shane has to go to the capitol in Salem for some training class for the program he's in, and Leo and I are going to tag along so we can come visit you.

I'm so excited to see you.

We will be there next Friday morning. I already called the prison and arranged the visit, maybe by the time you get this letter, you'll already know all of this.

But you told me to let you know, so I am.

Get that hair combed!

I can't wait to see you.

Forever,

December

* * *

DECEMBER,

Wow.

It was so good to see you.

I can't believe three years went by so fast.

You look older, as I told you. Not in your face or anything, but your eyes. I guess the same could be said of me, huh? Still, you look amazing, just as I expected.

Leo is absolutely adorable. I'm so happy I got to meet him. Leo would have loved your son, December. He loved you so much, too. He would have been an amazing uncle.

I'll be honest, seeing you was hard. It took me a few days to recover. I guess, being in here, it makes you look to the future, you know? At least for me. I promised myself I wouldn't dwell on the past, my first night in here. What's done was done and I just needed to get through my sentence so I could move on with my life.

But seeing you just reminded me of everything.

How everything used to be so easy. So fun. So damned carefree. The three of us were like family, well four, I guess, if you include Shane.

I miss that so much it hurts. We lost so much.

I miss you, December.

Thanks for coming to see me.
Forever,
Wolfe

* * *

WOLFE,

It was so good to see you, too.

It was hard for me, as well.

My parents are getting along a little better lately, so I've been spending more time at home. Shane's always gone, so it's just me and Leo and Lucy. But that just gives me more time to think and sometimes, that's not such a good thing, you know?

This is all so very hard and unfair.

There are so many times when I wish you hadn't confessed. I wish everything was different. I understand why you did it — so Leo would have his father around — but sometimes I wish you didn't.

Maybe that sucks for me to say, but it's the truth.

Life is not very pleasant for me lately. At least I have Leo, though.

And you.

And wine. Sometimes, I wouldn't make it through the night without my cabernet.

I'll write again soon, promise.

Forever,

December

* * *

DECEMBER,

Hey, girl, you doing okay?

Sorry it's been a few months since I wrote. Just been in my own head, trying to get through each day alive.

I don't know if you saw on the news or not, but there was a big riot in here a few weeks ago. A huge race war has broken out and everyone is

19

fighting with everyone. It's already tense as hell normally, but things have been worse lately.

So, yeah, just making it back to my cell at night without getting shanked is an accomplishment most days.

Anyway, in case you did see it, I just wanted to let you know I'm okay.

I hope you are, too.

Take it easy on that cabernet.

Forever,

Wolfe

* * *

WOLFE,

Hi.

God, it's been a year since I wrote and I feel awful about it.

Leo takes up every second of my day. He is constantly asking 'why' about everything.

Why is the sky blue?

Why is the light red?

Why are the potatoes hot?

Why do I have to sleep?

Why is Mommy crying?

Mommy is crying because she needs a nap, Leo!

Haha!

I swear, this boy is a ball of constantly moving energy that never seems to stop. You'd think he'd want to sleep, but no, it's just go go go!

Anyway, that's my sorry excuse for not writing sooner.

Also, the fact that I have nothing to write about. As I described above, there's not really anything exciting happening to me. I don't have time for anything else.

Leo's almost five now and he'll be in Kindergarten soon, so there's a possibility I'll have some time alone in the future. It'll only be half days, though. I guess I'll nap then?

Shane graduated from his program and he's a junior officer now. It's so weird seeing him in a cop's uniform. Honestly, it seems to have gone to his head, he's almost insufferable now. He's not home much, and I'm kind of grateful for that, because he's hard to take.

I shouldn't say that, because Leo misses him when he's not here.

What are you up to? Are you still taking classes?

Write me back and catch me up, okay?

Forever,

December

* * *

DECEMBER,

Hey. What's up?

I got your letter a few weeks ago, it was good to hear from you.

Yeah, I guess they say kids take up all your time and they were right, huh? I heard it gets a little easier as they get older. I hope you got your nap, though.

I don't want you to worry, but I got in a fight a few weeks ago and I got stabbed. I'm okay now, though. The wound got infected, and I had to spend a few nights in the hospital up the street, but now I'm back and I'm fine. It was kind of nice to get away, to be honest, even though I felt like shit. The nurses were nice. The doctors, not so much.

About Shane — make sure he's taking care of you and Leo. That means more than just giving you money, December. He already had a huge ego, so I'm not surprised it's worse now that he's got a badge to flash around. I worry about you two a lot.

Write back soon.

Miss you.

Forever,

Wolfe

* * *

WOLFE,

Hi!

21

Surprise, it's me! I know I haven't written in forever, but I just wanted to check in and say hello.

Leo's seven now, isn't that wild? He'll be starting second grade this year. I can hardly believe it myself.

We moved into a new house. It's nice. It's close to Leo's school and close to the Sheriff's office, so it's convenient.

Unfortunately, I have some bad news. My parents died a few months ago. I'm sorry I didn't write to tell you sooner, I just couldn't seem to bring myself to put it down on paper, for some reason. Mom fell again and never recovered. Not surprisingly, a month after she passed, Dad passed peacefully in his sleep one night. I always knew they'd never make it long without each other. It was kind of beautiful, to be honest. It brings me comfort knowing they're together forever now. He was so distraught after she passed.

Even though I don't have much time to write, I just wanted to tell you that I think about you often.

Forever,

December

* * *

December,

Hey there, girl.

How's everything in Depoe Bay?

It's been years since I've seen you. God, Leo must be nine now, huh? That means that you are now twenty-seven!

We're getting old, girl!

Haha.

I guess I am, too. I'm right behind you!

I'm grateful for the passing of time, though.

I'm up for a hearing next year and my lawyers say things are looking good. I was given fifteen years, but they think I'll be able to get out after serving ten and that's just around the corner.

I try not to get too excited about it, because anything could happen between now and then. It's hard not to fantasize, though. I have a bachelor's degree in Pre-law now, and I'm thinking about applying to law schools when or if I get out. We'll see.

The one thing I do know is that I don't want to go back to Depoe Bay. I think I'll stay on the coast, but move farther north. Maybe Newport Beach. Maybe Seaside, I always liked it there. Not that they have law schools there, but it might be a nice place to land temporarily while I figure everything out.

Maybe you and Leo could come visit sometime? You know, once I get a job and get settled?

It'd be real nice to see you both again.

I hope you're doing well, December.

Forever,

Wolfe

* * *

WOLFE,

The thought of you getting out of there makes me so happy I want to cry. I hope your hearing goes well. Please keep me posted.

I'll be praying that it does.

Forever,

December

* * *

DECEMBER,

The hearing did go well.

I'll be out of here in six months, as long as I can keep my nose clean till then. I can hardly believe it myself.

My mind is working overtime imagining everything I'm going to do when I get out. The first thing on my agenda is devouring a big, juicy steak at a nice restaurant. Damn, I miss steak. And a cold, frosty beer. My mouth waters just thinking about it right now.

I got a buddy who was released a while back. He's a biker in Southern Oregon. He says I can come down and prospect for them, if I want, once I'm out. I'm thinking about it. It's a far cry from applying to law schools, I know.

But it might be a good place to go, just for a little while, so I can figure things out.

I don't really have anywhere else to land, you know? It's not like the fucking state is going to give me money for an apartment or anything, so I have to figure something out, or I'll just be out on the streets. I'm not about to call my old man. I haven't heard from him, not once, the entire time I've been in here.

Anyway, I'll keep you posted.

Anything could happen.

Forever,

Wolfe

 OLFE

Snow crunched under my boots. The top layer, which had turned to ice overnight, snapped under my weight as I walked down the trail and headed towards the clubhouse.

I could already hear signs of life, despite the fact that dawn was barely breaking through the clouds overhead. The dark grey sky was a clear indicator that it was going to be another gloomy winter day here in the Tillamook Forest.

I zipped up my leather jacket as I rounded the corner, smiling when I saw through the window that someone had already started a fire inside. I stomped on the mat, trying to get off as much snow as possible from my heavy leather boots.

The door creaked as I pulled it open, the warmth of the flames blasting me in the face as soon as I stepped foot inside.

Lacey and Riot were in the kitchen, lovingly holding each other and swaying to the soft Christmas music drifting through the air, the smell of bacon and eggs making my stomach growl. Colorful, blinking lights were strewn up around the room, making the impending arrival of the holiday hard to ignore.

"Wolfe!" Riot said, untangling himself from his lovely lady.

"Morning," I nodded.

"Are you hungry?" Lacey asked, her pretty green eyes shining bright and happy.

"Starved!" I replied, pouring myself a cup of coffee as she pulled a plate from the cabinet and handed it to me.

"Help yourself, there's plenty," she said.

"You're the best," I said. Looking around the room as I sipped my coffee, I spotted Pepper and Storm snuggled up on the couch in front of the fire and couldn't help but smile. The two of them had been inseparable since Pepper joined us here and I couldn't be happier for Storm, who'd been my best buddy long before the two of us had joined up with the Gods of Chaos Motorcycle Club.

The things we did with the Goddamn Gentlemen, our previous club, were far behind us. I shuddered to think of the pain we'd caused.

But that was all over now.

Now, we're Gods. We're both so proud to be a part of Solid Ground — the organization that Grace and Ryder formed years ago to help those who couldn't turn to traditional sources of assistance.

Our work's dangerous and unpredictable, but to be honest, that's what makes it exciting. It's hard, don't get me wrong.

The pain I've seen in the eyes of survivor's would haunt me for the rest of my life.

But it was all worth it.

The knowledge that we weren't just wrecking havoc on the world for a payday anymore was amazing and the sense of accomplishment and honor we felt was something I'd never experienced in my life.

It was also something I wasn't sure I'd ever feel.

I spent ten years in the pen for a murder I didn't commit and they were the longest, hardest years of my life so far. I mean, yeah, it was my choice, so I'm not complaining, but that doesn't mean it was easy.

Prison hardened my heart. To survive, I had to become just as hard as everyone else in there. And I did. I built a wall so big around my heart that nobody can get inside. Probably not even me anymore.

It was for a good cause, or so I thought at the time, at least.

It's been years since I've heard from December, though, so I can only hope that she and little Leo are doing okay now. After I got out, I headed south to join up with the Gentlemen and our friendship just seemed to fade away. I haven't even seen them since I've been free.

I thought about heading back to Depoe Bay once I was released, but the thought of facing the past, driving past that damned convenience store on the interstate, seeing Shane again? Yeah, I had no interest in any of that.

I'd done nothing but think of the past the whole time I was locked up and once I was free, the past was the last thing I wanted to revisit. So, I called up my friend and told him I was ready to prospect, and the club welcomed me with open arms.

And even though being in that club hardened me even more, I was grateful to have a place — any place — to land.

As I filled my plate with bacon, eggs and biscuits this morning, and slowly sauntered over to sit with Storm and Pepper, I felt myself counting my blessings again, just as I did countless times a day.

A man like me doesn't usually get a second chance.

I knew how blessed I was and I wasn't about to forget it.

"Hey, buddy, how'd you sleep?" Storm asked, as he and Pepper scooted over to make room for me on the couch.

"Like a log, now that you aren't rattling the walls with your snoring," I joked, and it was true. Having an entire cabin to myself now that Pepper and Storm had moved into their own was like a dream come true. I'd never had my own place and I was really enjoying the privacy.

Sure, it was lonely but I was used to being alone.

I'd been alone all my life, practically. Except for that brief period of time when December, Leo, Shane and myself formed a little tribe of our own. That didn't last long, though, but I can still conjure up what it felt like if I try real hard.

I don't try very often, though, because that shit hurts.

To think of everything we lost. I mean, hell, maybe the only thing December and Shane lost was Leo, but I sure felt like I lost a lot more.

I had dreams back then. Hell, I had dreams when I was in prison, too.

But once I got out and joined up with an outlaw gang, the chances of becoming a successful lawyer just fell by the wayside. Not many people are too keen on giving an ex-con a job, let alone a job in a law firm.

I never in a million years thought I'd find a different way to fight injustice.

But being a God suited me much better. It was the best of both worlds, and I wasn't bound by the rule of law. I was still doing good in the world, and I guess, deep down, that's all I ever really wanted to do.

Hell, that's why I confessed to a crime I didn't commit in the first place.

Maybe it was foolish, or impulsive, or even useless in the end. After examining my decision from every angle, I knew that in that moment, I ran into that store for a myriad of reasons, but I wasn't really thinking clearly.

Mainly, I didn't believe Leo could really be dead.

But also, I was still reeling from the news of December's pregnancy. It was like our lives flashed before me in that moment, and all I could see was Shane going to jail, and since we were in the car with him, the possibility of me and December going to jail, too, was very real.

All I could think about was that baby, nestled innocently inside December's womb and not asking for any of that. I wanted to give him the best possible chance at a good life, and if that meant taking the rap, then I was okay with that.

Once I saw Leo was truly dead, I knew I couldn't run. I checked on the clerk, who was lying behind the counter, and saw he was also dead.

When the cops arrived just seconds later, they found me behind the counter, the gun at my feet. I didn't tell them that Shane or

December was ever there, because now that Leo was dead, I knew December didn't have anyone left in the world but me and Shane.

And I wasn't the father of that child.

Shane was.

That baby was going to need his mama and his daddy.

I did the only thing I thought was right, even if it felt all wrong.

Everything after they arrived is a big blur.

I confessed, they arrested me, and early the next morning, I was charged with both murders without even being questioned for too long. I kept my confession simple, so they would believe it. I told them we went to rob the store, things went sour, and I'd shot both Leo and the clerk when I panicked.

I'd somehow managed to think it all through on the way to the precinct and by the time they put me in an interrogation room, I had all the details worked out and they believed me. They even believed the clerk's gun was my own, never even checking for prints or gun residue.

It was a simple open and shut case for a bunch of very lazy investigators.

I was terrified, but I tried to be as strong as I could. I never let anyone see me cry, but there were plenty of tears that flowed when I was alone.

I cried for Leo.

I cried for December.

Fuck, I cried for me, too.

But I didn't let anyone know. To the world, I put on a brave face and I soldiered through it all. Once I got to prison in Salem, the only things that got me through were the friendship of my cell mate, Spike, and the letters from December. After a while, those became less and less frequent, but by then, I was used to life behind bars and I could tolerate things a little better.

I missed her like fucking crazy, though.

I never stopped loving her. I never stopped worrying about her. But I quickly realized that I'd given her over to Shane and that was a consequence of my decision that I couldn't change. All I could do was hope she learned to take care of herself.

The irony of Shane becoming a fucking cop wasn't lost on me. At the time, I was furious and disgusted. After a while, I guess I just stopped caring about what he did.

Not once did he reach out to me after that night. I wondered what he did with his gun, if it would turn up somehow and match up with the crime, but I never heard another word.

I took the rap for something he caused and he never thanked me, or even acknowledged it. And then he had the gall to become a cop. It was mind blowing.

I guess I just shut down after that. Trying to maintain a relationship with them all just seemed to take so much effort. And I knew December didn't want to hear what it was really like in that prison. If I told her the truth about how scary it really was, she'd have been racked with even more guilt and that wasn't why I took the rap.

I did it so she could be happy.

I did it so she could move on, as best as possible. Burdening her with my day-to-day reality wasn't going to do her any favors. So, I kept my letters vague and when they faded off to a trickle, I let them.

I took it as a sign that she was moving on and I figured that was a good thing. That's what I wanted.

And once I got out, I took it upon myself to do the same.

After more and more time passed, the thought of reaching out to her and little Leo seemed more and more awkward.

Now that Storm's all coupled up with Pepper, and happy as a damn clam, though, I found myself thinking about December more and more these days. I wondered about her. I wondered if she was still in Depoe Bay, what Leo was like.

Maybe it was the holidays that had me so nostalgic and sentimental, too, but it's been bad lately.

She seemed to be on my mind all the time.

As the morning wore on, the clubhouse filled up with my new tribe — sleepy-eyed and ready for breakfast — and I turned my thoughts to the present.

The past never served me well and that would never change.

What I had now? I cherished it every day, because I knew what the other side looked like and I had no intention of ever going back to that.

CHAPTER 3

 ECEMBER

FRANTIC AND PANICKED, I tore through Shane's apartment like a tornado, looking for any clue of where he may have gone. After convincing his landlord to let me in, I'd locked the door behind me and began searching through every drawer and closet, inspecting every scrap of paper I could find.

It took me an hour before I found what I was looking for.

"You bastard!" I cried, my hands trembling as I looked down at the title for a boat, recently registered in Shane's name. That had to be where they were.

I'd already searched through his bank account online, hoping a charge for a hotel somewhere might show up. But other than a large transfer to another account, one which I didn't have access to, on the day he left, there were no other transactions after that.

He was doing his best to hide from me and it was working. Now, I knew why — because he and Leo were most likely hiding on his newly purchased boat.

It's been three days since he kidnapped Leo. He had his normally scheduled visit for the weekend, but when he didn't bring him back home to me on Sunday night, I knew something was wrong.

I called him incessantly for twenty-four hours.

Then, I called the cops. Of course, that was useless, and I knew that was going to be the case, but I had to try. Shane was buddies with everyone on the force, he was their golden boy, for fuck's sake. He'd quickly risen in the ranks to become one of the Lincoln County Chief's favorites and I didn't even want to know what he did to get there.

Two of Shane's buddies showed up after I called — Carl and Eddie — sauntering up the sidewalk without a care in the world while I tore my hair out with worry. They laughed. They joked. They made excuses. Surely, Shane was just taking a few extra days with the boy, they'd said, no need to panic, miss.

I wanted to strangle them by the time they left, and it was clear as day I was going to get no help at all finding my son.

So, I took things into my own hands. I scoured his bank and cell phone records online, hoping I'd find them that way. When that didn't work, I drove down every single road in Depoe Bay, then did the same with the neighboring towns. The whole time, all I could do was imagine the worst.

And then, I received an email from Shane, clearly stating his intentions, which left me shuddering with fear.

Shane never loved Leo. Once he was born, it was like he resented him and he was just gone all the time. He never took the time to bond with him, but he used him as a pawn in his life whenever it was convenient. It looked good to have an old lady and son at home. Every proper cop had a family. It was like being a politician. It was all for show, mostly.

Eventually, I finally had enough and I kicked him out. He was furious, because that did not look good for him. Once he got his own place, we decided he would have visitation of Leo every other weekend and I was actually happy about it.

It meant I would have some much needed time alone.

I never in a million years thought it would come to this.

The last year has allowed Shane to build up a huge resentment against me, especially once I wouldn't let him come home, despite his begging. His anger towards me grew to a boiling rage and now it's spilled over onto our son and I can't believe I didn't see this coming.

His email was very clear. He insisted he was doing this to hurt me as much as he possibly could. He promised I'd never see Leo again.

I had no disillusions about what he meant by that.

He wouldn't hesitate to hurt him, just to break me.

That's why I knew I had to work fast. I had to find him before he could do that.

But a damned boat?

How was I supposed to find him now? Tears rolled down my face as I regretted ever meeting Shane in the first place. He was not the person I was meant to be with. My life wasn't supposed to be like this.

Everything had gone wrong.

Except Leo. He was everything to me. He was all I had.

And I knew there was no way in hell I could live without him. I knew I had to do whatever it took to find him. I knew I'd never stop looking.

My problem was I didn't know where to start.

I took a deep breath and tried to slow my mind — to think.

I thought about my brother, Leo, and what he would do in this situation. Living without my twin brother had been so hard. I'd always looked to him to help guide me through life. This last decade had left me feeling like I was just lost, going through the motions with no real destination.

If he were here now, he'd have called up his best friend, Wolfe, and they would have figured this all out together, forming a relentless team until the problem was solved.

Maybe I didn't have my brother anymore to reach out to, but Wolfe was still an option, even though it's been years since I talked to him. His old man was still living in the same house he'd lived in all these years. Maybe he'd give me his phone number, if he had it?

I pocketed the boat title and left Shane's apartment in shambles as I ran out to my car.

Leo was everything. Maybe Wolfe couldn't help me. Maybe he would refuse to help me, after all these years, after everything he's been through. And that would be perfectly understandable.

But for my boy's sake, I had to try.

CHAPTER 4

 OLFE

WHEN MY OLD man's name popped up on my phone, it surprised me. I hadn't heard from him in years, not since I called him after getting out of the pen. I'd updated him on my move to the northern part of the state after moving and that was about it. I'd never forgiven him for basically disowning me. I doubt if I ever will. I'd never told him I didn't actually kill anyone. Why should I explain if he was going to disown me anyway?

I almost didn't answer.

But curiosity got the best of me, and I hit the green button, allowing his voice to come ringing in my ears, as familiar as always.

"Hey, Pop," I answered.

"How are you doing, son?"

"Fine, fine, getting along. How about you?" I asked, thinking someone must have died, or he was going to tell me he had some fatal disease, a sick feeling forming in my gut. Why else would he call after all this time?

"Oh, I'm getting old, son, but that's to be expected. My back is shot. My knees, too. Arthritis, mostly. I've been lucky, though, so far. Knock on wood."

"That's good, Pop," I replied.

"You still up north?"

"Yep," I answered, not offering any other details. As far as I was concerned, he didn't deserve a window into my life. He hadn't earned it.

"Good, good," he said, pausing just long enough to make me wonder if he was having regrets in his old age. "Listen, son, I got a visit. I wasn't sure if it was okay to pass your number along, so I got her number instead."

"A visit?"

"Yeah, from your old friend, December. The one who's birthday is in June," he chuckled. He'd always thought that was the funniest thing.

"Oh." Hearing December's name come out of his mouth threw me a little. Hell, I hadn't said her name out loud in years myself. But the fact that she was so heavily on my mind this morning made perfect sense now. "How is she doing?"

"She didn't seem good, son," he said. "I got her number to pass along. She really wants to talk to you."

"Okay," I nodded, slowly, my heart picking up a beat. What could December want after all these years? "Let me get a pen."

I ran into the clubhouse and grabbed a pen and paper and walked back out to the porch swing and sat down. "Go ahead."

I scribbled her number down before we said a quick, brief good-bye, not even a wistful exchange of affection passing between us.

So be it.

Wanting privacy, I walked back to my cabin before dialing December's number. My fingers trembled as I punched her number into my phone, my heart beating like a drum in my chest.

I took a deep breath, steeling myself.

She answered on the first ring, her voice like a jolt right back into the past.

"Wolfe?"

"Hey, girl."

I closed my eyes, wanting all my senses to be focused on her and her alone.

"Thanks for calling," she said, her voice shaky.

"Of course," I answered. "What's going on, are you okay?"

She paused, sighing, and in my head, I could see her bite her bottom lip, just as she always did when she was about to say something important, just as she did that night before she told me she was pregnant.

"I don't know if I should have reached out or not, but I need your help."

"Okay," I said, prodding her to continue.

"It's Leo. Or Shane. Well, both, really. Shane took him. Leo. I think — I think he's going to hurt them, Wolfe," she said, her voice cracking.

"Hurt them?" I asked, my eyes flying open.

"Leo has Lucy, our dog, with him, too."

"I see. Where are you? Where are they?"

"I'm in Depoe Bay, and that's the thing. I don't know where they are. Shane bought a boat without telling me, and I think they may be on it."

"Why do you think he's going to hurt them?"

"He sent me an email saying just that."

I paused, taking it all in, my head spinning. If Shane hurt that boy, he was a dead man.

"How can I help?"

"Honestly, I don't know if you can. I'm just so alone, Wolfe. My parents died, and Leo is all I have now."

"Did you call the cops?"

"Of course!" She cried. "But Shane's still a cop, too, and they aren't taking me seriously. He's good at pretending to be a good family man. He's anything but."

"I see," I nodded, finally understanding.

"I probably shouldn't have called..." Her voice sounded so small and sad that it broke my heart. It didn't take but about three seconds to figure out what I needed to do.

38

"I'm on my way."

CHAPTER 5

ECEMBER

THOSE FOUR LITTLE words brought me so much comfort I was almost ashamed. I had no right looking for comfort from Wolfe. He'd given up so much for us already. His entire life.

But when I said he was all I had, it was the truth. And shame be damned, I was ecstatic he was coming. Staying still was close to impossible, so I spent the next few hours pacing and cleaning my house as I waited for him, the snow falling heavily outside my window.

I couldn't help but wonder what he would be like.

What he would look like.

If he hated me...

But would he have so quickly offered to come down if that were the case? I hoped not.

I knew he felt obligated to us because of his loyalty to my brother. But hadn't he paid those dues already, if he ever really owed them to begin with? I'm pretty sure Leo would have wanted to see Shane go to prison for shooting the clerk instead of Wolfe. I often wondered what Leo would have thought about Wolfe taking the blame for all of that. He probably would have hated it.

Maybe none of that mattered anymore.

Damn, it was good to hear his voice, though. My stomach flipped and twisted in anticipation.

I took a shower and dressed, taking a little extra care with my appearance. It'd been years since I'd seen Wolfe that one time I visited him in Salem, and my heart fluttered at the thought.

I'd always had feelings for Wolfe. I'd buried them way down long ago, or so I thought. Now that he was on his way, they were all bubbling to the surface whether I wanted them to or not.

I smiled as I put on a little bit of mascara, remembering the one time we'd kissed. My god, we'd been so young. I was barely sixteen and it was just the one time, but I'd never forgotten it. I had a huge crush on him, and I hoped that kiss would lead to more, but it never did. He never said why, but I suspected Leo disapproved and Wolfe didn't want to disrespect him.

He was always so damned honorable.

Sighing, I stared at myself in the mirror, wondering what Wolfe would see when he arrived. Did I look the same as he remembered? I felt tired and full of sorrow and worry and when I looked at my reflection, that's all I saw.

I tucked my dark hair behind my ears and shook my head.

"That's as good as it's going to get today," I said out loud, as I turned off the bathroom light and headed to the couch to wait for him.

He's a different person now, I reminded myself, as I flipped on the television. He may be nothing like I remembered. And maybe I'm nothing like he remembers — and that's okay.

I was just thankful he was coming.

CHAPTER 6

OLFE

THE DRIVE down the 101 was cold and treacherous. About halfway there, I realized I should have borrowed one of the club's SUVs instead of hopping on my Harley, but it was too late by then.

I'd just have to barrel through.

The drive that would normally take me just over an hour took almost three hours instead.

By the time I got to Depoe Bay, I was frozen solid.

Just as well, because as soon as I rolled across the Lincoln County line, the memories of my life here began flooding my brain. It was best I concentrate on the painful frigid temperatures instead of the painful memories that surrounded me. When I passed the scene of the crime all those years ago, I kept my focus on the road and refused to even look at it.

I found December's house easily, the layout of the tiny town etched into my brain. Slowly, I rolled to a stop on her street, taking in the small Tudor house in front of me. It was a nice place and I was glad Leo had a good home to grow up in. My rage at Shane had been simmering inside of me and the fact that he'd given them a good home to live in didn't make that subside any. It was the least he could have done.

I walked down the snow-covered sidewalk, brushing the snow off my shoulders as I removed my helmet and ran a hand through my hair. I was drenched and probably not looking my best, but I'd wanted to get here so quickly, I didn't care about any of that.

Not like I had much to work with. What you see is what you get when it comes to me. I was hoping December was willing to overlook that.

I admonished myself, shaking my head, as I rang her doorbell. Her son was missing, the last thing she was going to be thinking about was what my ugly mug looked like.

The door opened and it was like a light lit up in my heart.

"December," I whispered, a smile stretching across my face.

"Hey," she said, smiling back, her eyes shining brightly into mine. She threw open the door and invited me in and I stepped in hesitantly. The house was cozy and warm and neat and tidy, with a fire roaring in the fireplace. "You look so cold!"

"Yeah, I'm on my bike," I said.

"Bike?" She looked up at me like I was crazy.

"Motorcycle," I clarified, sliding off my wet leather jacket and heading over to her fireplace. I wanted the warmth of the fire, but I also needed to put some distance between us. I wanted to pull her into my arms and hug her but I was afraid letting go would prove almost impossible.

She looked so damned good.

Her hair was long now, dark and straight and falling around her shoulders. She looked older than I remembered, but the years looked good on her, lending a maturity and fullness to her face that wasn't there before. Her smile faded pretty quickly as she walked over and faced me as I stood next to the fire.

"Can I get you anything? Are you hungry?"

"Something to drink would be great," I said.

"Ice tea? Coffee?"

"Got any whiskey?"

"Oh," she said, her eyes widening. "Yeah, I think so."

She padded off and rummaged around in the kitchen and I took a moment to look around. There were pictures of her and Leo on the mantle, so I grabbed one and looked closer. Leo looked just like his Mom, which meant he also looked like his Uncle Leo. It was a bit unnerving and I quickly put the photo back. I scanned the room and only found one picture of Shane, shoved in the back of a corner bookshelf by the front door. He looked older, harder, almost angrier, if that was even possible.

December came back and we sat on the couch together as I sipped my whiskey.

"I can't believe you came," she said, her knees bobbing up and down nervously.

"Yeah?" I asked, raising a brow. "Why not?"

She shrugged and looked away, staring into the flames. The amber glow lit up her skin and she looked like an angel of fire sitting next to me. I resisted the urge to reach out and touch her.

"I don't really deserve your friendship."

"What makes you say that?"

"So much time has passed," she said, turning back to me, her eyes searching mine.

"I know," I agreed. "I appreciate that. Without all that time passing, I wouldn't be here."

"Right," she nodded, squaring her shoulders. "I barely wrote. I only visited once. You deserved better..."

"Well, that's more than anyone else did," I said, flashing her a wry smile.

"Still," she replied, shaking her head.

"Listen, December. I don't care about the past. I'm here to help you, but I'm going to need a little more information, okay? But I'm going to be perfectly honest with you, too. I'm not the same person I used to be."

"I guess that makes two of us," she said.

44

"Then I guess we're going to have to get to know each other all over again."

"I'd like that," she said, biting her lip.

"Me, too," I said, reaching out and grabbing her hand. She turned her palm up, our fingers intertwining. My heart pounded in my chest as I looked into her eyes. She looked so scared.

"Everything's going to be okay," I said. "We're going to find them."

"I hope so," she said, her voice quivering.

Throwing caution to the wind, I pulled her into my arms.

I did it to comfort her, but a wave of emotion washed over me, a wave so big it threatened to break me down completely. Tears sprang to my eyes and I realized how very much I needed to hug this woman. Not just tonight. But I'd needed it for years. I'd needed it since the moment Shane jumped into the car with us. I'd needed it since my feet hit the pavement and I ran into that store. I'd needed it since I'd sat through the sentencing hearing with her cries echoing through the hallowed halls of that courthouse.

I'd needed it since I heard the loud clang of my cell doors closing — every single day for a decade.

She leaned into me and I felt her shaking. Blinking away my own tears before they could fall, I held her close and stroked her hair. After a moment, she pulled away, her brown eyes brimming with intensity as she peered into mine.

"Leo is everything to me," she hissed, her voice thick with urgent emotion.

"I know," I whispered. "I know."

"I can't live through —."

"Shhh, don't," I said, shaking my head. "You won't have to. I promise."

I reached up, wiping a tear off her cheek with my thumb. Her eyes were glued to mine and I felt the connection that had always been there between us reappear and we both smiled at the same time.

"I missed you so much," she said.

I nodded slowly. "Me, too, December."

We gazed at each other for a few moments, but I knew that this time, time was not on our side and not to be wasted.

"Now, listen. I need you to tell me everything, okay? Don't leave anything out."

"Okay," she nodded, pulling herself out of my arms and sitting up, leaving me feeling an unexpected emptiness. "It's not good, Wolfe."

"I gathered as much. Don't leave anything out."

She steeled herself, biting her lip before beginning and I fought off a feeling of deja vu as I focused on her every word.

"Shane never stopped being Shane. After we left the store that night, we drove up and down the coast until the sun came up. I must have cried the whole time. He was silent for most of it. Just driving. At some point, I fell asleep and when I woke up, we were parked off in the woods and Shane was burning his clothes. He'd washed himself off with some water we had in the back of the car. When he got back in, he told me we needed to get our stories straight. It was my birthday, you probably remember, so he said we'd say we wanted to be alone and that we spent the whole night at the beach alone. I agreed, and then he just started acting like nothing happened. He drove me back home and the cops were there telling my parents that Leo had died and you'd confessed. Shane and I stuck to the story and that was that. Nobody even asked us any questions.

"After a few weeks, I told him I was pregnant. He was pissed, at first. But he came around after a while and apologized. With both you and Leo gone, I felt like I had no choice. I needed him. Or so I thought. Turns out, I've done most everything by myself anyway, so I didn't need him to help raise Leo after all."

I took a deep breath, pushing away the feeling that I'd done all that time behind bars for nothing. Shane had not stepped up in the way I hoped. That much was obvious.

"After that, things just fell into place, I guess. Not with me and Shane, we never really had much of a relationship. But I just kept going. Leo was a delight, so I had him and that was enough, I guess. But after Shane became a cop, he got even worse. He started…"

She stopped, staring at me with hesitation.

"What?"

She broke our gaze, looking away.

"Our arguments got worse. He was pissed, because I started taking classes at the community college in Lincoln City," she shrugged.

"That's great," I said.

"Yeah, I'm going to be a nurse," she said, pausing before continuing. "But Shane hated the fact that he had to watch Leo for me while I was gone. So, we argued, constantly. He'd take it out on me, but also on Leo. One night, it got particularly bad. First, he started spanking Leo, which upset me and when I tried to get him to stop, he turned on me."

"He hit you, too?"

She nodded, tears springing to her eyes again. "Yeah. I'd already kicked him out. But since then, he's gotten angrier and angrier and I've been so scared to let him see Leo, but I didn't have a choice. He would pick him up after school without telling me, scaring the shit out of me. After a while, I realized it was just easier to let him visit regularly, as much as I hated it. I made him promise never to lay a hand on Leo again. But now he's done this. I never should have let him near him."

Rage bubbled up inside of me that I struggled to contain. I rose to my feet, walking over to the fire and looking into the flames. I didn't want her to see how angry I was. My chest rose and fell, as if the fury pulsed through the very air I was breathing.

"Tell me about the email."

Slowly, I turned around, smiling gently at her, to the best of my ability.

"He's crazy, Wolfe. He didn't bring Leo home when he was supposed to, so I called and called, but he never answered. I went to the police station, but they blew me off. After that, I got an email saying he'd taken Leo away and because I'd gone to see the Sheriff, and humiliated him, he was taking Leo away and never bringing him back, to punish me."

I nodded, taking it all in. Shane was a sonofabitch and fantasies of ripping his fucking head off were dancing through my head.

"Is that it?"

"No."

"What else?"

"It was his words. Here, I'll read it to you," she said, jumping up and grabbing her laptop. She pulled it up and started reading, her voice shaking. "December, you've gone too far. Reporting me to the Sheriff was your biggest mistake. Were you trying to humiliate me? You've only hurt yourself. Leo's mine now. I know he's the only thing you care about. So, consider him lost at sea. Have fun drowning in your sorrows, you ungrateful bitch. Love, Shane."

She closed the laptop and looked over at me.

"What a prick," I said, my teeth grinding together.

"I wasn't sure what he meant, until I broke into his house and found this." She pulled a folded-up piece of paper from her pocket and gave it to me. I opened it up and saw it was a title for a boat in Shane's name.

I handed it back to her, my mind spinning.

"I think it's time I told you a little about what I've been doing the last few years," I said.

She looked at me with a curious glance and smiled.

"Okay," she said, settling back on the cushion. "I'm all ears."

CHAPTER 7

ECEMBER

HE WASN'T *anything* like I remembered.

Even when I'd seen him in jail, he resembled something of the young man I once knew, but now?

It was like his soul had inhabited a completely different body.

He was huge, first of all. His arms were as big as my thighs. Ripped and slathered in tattoos, he moved through my house with the confidence of a lion.

His tight Levi's clung to his muscular ass and the black leather vest he wore, with patches on the front and back, made him look like he'd just walked off the silver screen, some mysterious character with thrilling stories to tell. His black hair was peppered with generous amounts of grey, making him look older than he was.

When he wrapped those massive arms around me, I'd never felt safer in my entire life.

His somber eyes held those stories, deep and dark, and I wondered at the depths of what he'd seen, what he'd lived through.

And he'd done it all for me and my son. It was almost too much to take. That's why I'd let the distance fall between us over the years. I'd never be able to repay him and truth be told, I'd regretted that he'd done it.

Maybe if he had let Shane take the fall, like he'd deserved, things would have worked out differently between me and Wolfe. Maybe I'd have felt safe every night since, falling asleep in his arms.

But I'd never know.

The cards had fallen and there was no going back now.

"After I got out, I joined up with a group of bikers. Outlaw bikers. The Goddamned Gentlemen. I think I mentioned in a letter that a buddy of mine was already a member, so I prospected for them and moved up the ranks pretty quick. It was hard work. It was dangerous. I did shit that I easily could have been thrown back behind bars for, but I was never caught. Unfortunately, shit blew up for the club's president and the whole thing fell apart. But that's where things actually got good."

"What do you mean?"

"Most of my club joined up with another club. The Gods of Chaos. They aren't like other clubs, December. They're outlaws, sure, but they're good guys. And they're not just guys, there are women involved, too."

"Women bikers?" I asked, intrigued.

"Sort of," he said, smiling. "You'd love them, December. Grace and Ryder, they're our leaders, they started this organization — it's called Solid Ground and all of the Gods are a part of it. They do all kinds of things, but their mission is to help people out of situations when they can't find help otherwise."

"What do you mean?"

"Well, like Lacey. She was sold to the Mayor of Seattle by her mother when she was a young teen. He kept her prisoner, made her do things nobody should have to do. But, because of his power, she couldn't call the cops. So, Solid Ground helped her get away."

I nodded, drinking it all in.

"We get all kinds of jobs, though. Sometimes, it's an entire group of people we have to help. It can get dangerous, at times. But it's worth it. And, if we can help the survivors get a little closure, maybe even a little revenge, then it's even more rewarding, in my opinion."

"Wow," I replied, sincerely impressed.

"I'm really glad I hooked up with them," he said. I could see the satisfaction in his eyes and I realized that the confidence I saw in him now was most likely tied to the Gods. He was doing good work and he was happy with himself.

"I'm happy for you," I said, the tightness in my chest loosening just a bit. I'd been weighed down by guilt for so long, it was nice to see his life wasn't completely ruined because of Shane, or me and Leo.

"I'm telling you all of this because I want you to have the confidence that I do that we're going to find Leo."

"What do you mean?"

"The Gods have a world of resources at our disposal. Riot, our computer guy, is a goddamn genius."

"Do you think they'll help me?"

"I know they will," he said, his blue eyes shining into mine. "All I have to do is make a phone call and the full force of the Gods will be unleashed upon Shane. He'll never know what hit him."

For the first time since I read Shane's email, a glimmer of hope lit up inside my heart.

I desperately wanted to believe him.

"I'm so glad I called you," I said, tears springing to my eyes.

He pulled me into his arms again and I felt like I could live there forever.

"So am I," he whispered, his arms tightening around me.

CHAPTER 8

HANE

"SHE'S CRAZY," I said, pressing the phone to my ear, struggling to hear the Sheriff over the wind coming off the ocean. "We're fine. Just fine."

"That's what I figured," he replied, with a laugh.

"The thing is, Chief, she's been neglecting the boy. She's always off at school, and I'm pretty sure she's stopping off at the bar after her classes. She doesn't get home till late, and he needs more than that, you know? Sorry for just running off like that without telling you. We just need a few days away, a little father-son bonding time, you know? Taking the boat out for the first time. Gonna head up North."

"Of course, of course, Shane," he said. "Take a whole week, Shane, you've earned it! Take care of your boy. Don't forget to send me your float plan, though, just in case. It's not the best time to be on a boat in the Pacific. Cold as hell…"

"Sure, sure," I said, smiling and nodding, even though he couldn't see me. My plan was working just fine. December could try, but she'd never succeed in bringing me down. Nobody would ever believe her over me. Since joining the force, I was seen as an upstanding member of our community. My reputation was stellar and when I did slip up — like that one time I got caught in a hotel room in Portland with a hooker, or that time I wrecked my truck after a few too many at the pub — my colleagues helped me sweep it all under the rug.

That's just what we did for each other.

None of us were perfect, but it was important that those on the outside certainly thought so.

"Thanks, Chief," I replied, hanging up the phone.

When I turned around, Leo was standing there looking at me.

"Why did you say that about Mom?" he demanded. He was getting older now, and he was growing his own little set of balls. I was almost impressed he had the courage to stand up to me, but he should know better than that.

"You shouldn't listen to my phone calls," I said, instantly irritated. I opened a browser on my phone and started filling out the float plan to email to the Chief.

"Well, I did," he said, his hands on his hips, his stupid dog wagging her tail next to him. The two of them were inseparable and had been ever since I brought her home. I'd done it out of a misplaced sliver of guilt after having a one-night stand with a girl from the bar I was working at and regretted it ever since. The dog ate too much, she peed on everything, and to be honest, she was a little bitch. We did not get along. "So?"

"Look, Bud, just go read your book, okay?"

"I don't know why you're lying about Mom. You're the one at the bar all the time and always out late."

He was getting on my last nerve. Hell, everything was these days.

"Sometimes you don't even come home at all!"

I closed the distance between us, getting in his face and ignoring Lucy's growl.

"Shut up, Leo!" I seethed. "Go read your fucking book — now!"

He sighed and turned to walk away, the dog following, but not before glaring at me over his shoulder.

Let him be mad, what did I care?

His mother spoiled him. I trusted December to take care of him and teach him how to respect his elders and he thinks it's okay to talk to me like that?

Fuck both of them!

I walked to the kitchen and grabbed a beer, popping it open and walking out of the cabin and onto the deck of the boat. The sun was setting in the distance and the waves gently rocked the boat. It was beautiful, if I could only relax enough to enjoy it. We'd docked for the night near Pacific City, after traveling all day.

It felt good to be away from the bullshit of my day-to-day life. Being a cop had perks, but it was also a pain in the ass. I always had to watch my back and keep up appearances and it was fucking exhausting. Sometimes, I just wanted to let myself go, have a few beers, invite over a couple of chicks, turn up the music, do some blow and just let loose.

Not that I could do any of that now, not with the boy so close by. He watched me like a fucking hawk.

Not for long, though.

Soon, I'd be done with the suffocating responsibility of being a father and December will be as miserable as she's made me all these years. And then, I'll be free as a fucking bird.

Revenge was going to be so sweet.

CHAPTER 9

EO

Lucy snuggled into my side as I curled up in bed. I pretended to read, just in case Dad came in but I couldn't concentrate at all.

I hated being on that stupid boat.

Maybe it would have been fun if Mom was there. I was worried about her, and after hearing Dad lie to the Chief like that, I knew something wasn't right.

Things haven't really been right in a long time, though. Maybe they were when I was really little, but I can barely remember that now.

All I really remember is Mom being sad all the time. The only times she really smiled was when she was talking to me, or talking about my Uncle Leo.

I'm named after him, but I never got to meet him. He died before I was born. He's my Mom's twin, so I bet I'd have liked him a lot. Is it possible to miss someone you never met before?

Mom talks about him so much, that sometimes it feels like I did know him. She talks about her friend Wolfe, too. She says we went to meet him once, but I don't remember. She has a picture of all three of them that she keeps in her wallet, and they all look so happy.

I wish I'd been alive back then, because it sure sounds like they had a lot of fun.

Lately, I haven't really had much fun at all. I keep getting shuttled back and forth between my house with Mom and Dad's new apartment. I'd rather just stay home, but I guess I don't have a say in it.

At least not for a few years.

Mom told me once I turn eighteen, I won't have to go to Dad's anymore, if I don't want to. Six years seems like a long time to wait to have an opinion on what I want to do and it just doesn't seem fair at all.

It's not that I don't love my dad. It's just that he's not very nice. I wish he was. I wish a lot of things, though, and not much of anything ever comes true.

The older I get, the more I learn how sad life is, you know?

I wonder if it will ever get better.

CHAPTER 10

OLFE

I HUNG up the phone and turned back to December. She stood in the kitchen listening, carefully sipping her wine. My conversation with Riot had gone well and I was confident he was going to get the ball rolling. I'd given him December's address and all the information he needed about Shane. In the morning, a few more Gods would get on the road and join us.

"They'll be here tomorrow," I said.

"They?"

"He's sending a few guys," I shrugged. "Strength in numbers."

Her eyes widened as she looked around. "I don't have a lot of room, but —."

"No worries, we'll get hotel rooms."

"Oh. Right," she nodded. She took a sip of wine and I walked over to her. She looked tired and incredibly stunning, all at the same time. The urge to protect her and reassure her was something I couldn't ignore. I grabbed her arms and peered into her eyes.

"We're going to find them, I promise," I said.

"Thank you," she replied, her voice a soft whisper in the quiet kitchen.

"You'll be amazed at what Riot, and all of the Gods, can accomplish," I said.

"I trust you, Wolfe," she confessed, my heart swelling with pride at her words. Her trust meant a lot to me.

"In the meantime, it's getting late. When's the last time you ate?"

She flashed me a guilty smile and shook her head. "I honestly can't remember."

"That's what I thought," I said. "Grab a warm jacket and some gloves."

"Where are we going?"

"You tell me," I laughed. "I haven't been here in a while. Whatever's open."

"Got it," she said, pulling away and heading to the closet by her front door. I grabbed my jacket, shrugging it on as I watched her. My eyes trailed over her body and I felt desire swell inside of me. She'd always been a knock-out, but now that the years had filled out her curves, there was a little more to feast my eyes on, and I was enjoying it immensely.

Maybe too much.

Bundled up, we walked out to my bike together and I unlocked my spare helmet and gave it to her to put on.

"I have a car we could use," she said, looking at me in confusion. The snow was falling steadily around us, leaving a heavy blanket on the ground.

"I prefer to stay out of cages as much as possible, if you don't mind," I said.

"Oh," she nodded, before smiling. "Okay then!" She pulled the helmet on and zipped up her coat as I straddled the bike. She jumped on behind me and wrapped her arms around my waist, her body pressed tight up against mine.

The breath seemed to be trapped inside of me, her arms and body wrapped around me leaving me momentarily paralyzed with emotion. For all the walls I'd built around my heart and emotions, she sure was piercing through them like they were made of the sheerest paper.

I started up the bike, forcing air through my lungs as it roared to life.

CHAPTER 11

ECEMBER

AS NERVOUS AS I was about driving through town on the back of a bike in the snow, I was just as grateful for the opportunity to wrap my entire body around Wolfe and hold on for dear life.

He was warm. His shoulders were wide. And his body was hard as a rock under that thick leather jacket. I rested my head on his upper back and squeezed harder, never wanting to let go.

I didn't even notice the cold. Or the wind. And if anyone else was on the road with us, I didn't notice them either.

Being in Wolfe's presence made it hard to think. I knew I needed to concentrate on finding Leo, but Wolfe left my heart racing and my head spinning.

We pulled up to Gracie's Sea Hag, a little oceanfront seafood place that had been there forever. Reluctantly, I let go of my grip on Wolfe, and pulled myself off the bike. We took our helmets and he smiled down at me, his eyes as warm as honey.

"I remember this place," he said. "Been here many times."

"Some things never change, I guess," I replied.

He chuckled and nodded, as we walked inside. As soon as we opened the door, we were blasted by the heat of the fireplace and the sound of Christmas music streaming through the crackling speakers.

Gracie herself greeted us, now well into her seventies. We sat at a table by the window, the mighty waves of the Pacific crashing below us, lights from the shore reflected off of her darkness.

Sitting across from Wolfe at a restaurant seemed almost surreal. I reached down and pinched my thigh, to remind myself that it wasn't a dream.

We ordered a couple of clam chowders, shrimp cocktail and fish n' chips and a few drinks, before Gracie walked off, but not before throwing a curious glance my way.

"I don't think she recognizes you," I said to Wolfe. Hell, I probably wouldn't have recognized himself if I'd just passed him on the street.

"That's just fine with me," he laughed, a loud roaring laugh that drew stares from the other diners.

"Thanks for bringing me here," I said. "You were right, I'm starving."

He shrugged. "Me, too. And if we're going to get your boy back, we have to take care of ourselves so we can do just that."

"I almost didn't call you," I said, smiling over at him. I wanted to drink in every inch of him, engrave the memory of his eyes and his smile into my brain.

"I'm glad you did," he said. "You may have thought I was far away, but I was always just a phone call away."

"I guess so," I agreed. "Thanks for that, too."

"Being here, despite the reason, is my pleasure, December. It's been way too long."

"It has," I nodded, swallowing hard. I didn't want to cry but my emotions were so raw and every time he looked at me with those gentle eyes, it made me want to just dissolve into a puddle of tears.

Tears for everything that went wrong.

Tears for all the possibilities that never had a chance.

After Gracie brought our drinks and I'd had a few sips, I decided it was time to get some things off my chest.

"Wolfe," I whispered. He'd been looking out the window into the darkness, and I could have watched him all day. But the liquid courage was kicking in and it was important.

"Yes?" He said, throwing that gentle smile my way again.

"I could apologize all day, but what I really want to say is that…I just wish I'd been with you that day."

"We were together," he said, cocking his head.

"That's not what I mean. I mean, together together."

"Oh," he nodded.

"I always liked you. I certainly liked you more than Shane. But after Leo freaked out so hard, just because we…" My voice trailed off and I felt a blush rush to my cheeks.

"Because we kissed?" he prodded.

My eyes crashed into his and a storm of memories washed over me. Suddenly, I could feel his lips on mine, the heat of our connection, the savage urge to kiss him again bringing me back to the present.

"Yes," I continued, my breath catching. "Because we kissed. If Leo hadn't objected, I think we might have had something good."

He nodded, slowly, my words hanging in the air between us.

"I think you're probably right, December."

I sighed, the weight of reality heavy on my shoulders.

"Damn you, Leo," I said softly, smiling over at him.

"I never understood why he'd approve of Shane and not me," Wolfe said.

"I think he was afraid it would screw up the friendship the three of us shared."

"Yeah, probably," he said. "I think he was wrong."

"I guess we'll never know."

"No, we won't," he said, looking away. He sighed before looking back at me. "I don't like to dwell on the past too much, December. It's too painful. It's a waste of time. And nothing good really happened in the past…not after that night, at least. The last few years have been great for me, though, and I do my best to stay anchored in the present."

"Makes sense," I said.

"But you know what?" he asked. The candlelight from the table's centerpiece lit up his eyes and with every word, it was like I was hypnotized. I wanted to know everything about him. I wanted to hear every word he had to say, I wanted to drink him in and never stop absorbing whatever he offered.

"What?"

"That stuff doesn't matter anymore."

"What does matter?"

"Right now," he nodded firm. "This moment. You, sitting across the table from me, the Christmas lights shimmering in your hair, your smile. Our friendship."

"Friendship, right," I nodded.

He reached across the table, grabbing my hand, his eyes intense and stormy.

"I'm not one to lie, December. I'm also not one to hold anything back. I know you're going through the worst time of your life right now, so maybe all of this is inappropriate and the worst timing in the world, but I've never been good at that sort of thing." He squeezed my hand, his warmth sending a shudder through my bones. "But since we're talking about regrets, I'll tell you what I regret. I regret listening to Leo when he asked me to back off. I regret not kissing you again. I regret taking the fall for Shane, or ever for a second thinking he would step up and be the man required to be a proper father to Leo. More than anything, I regret not telling you all those years ago how I felt about you."

"Oh," I said, my heart racing wildly at his words. It was like everything I wanted to hear, all at once. "How did you feel?"

"I loved you, December. We used to say that all the time, didn't we? Forever, right?"

"Forever," I whispered.

"But when I said it, I think I meant something different than you did. We were friends, always, but I loved you as more than that.

63

Things turned out the way they did, but that love I had for you never stopped. And maybe you didn't feel that way, too, and that's okay, but —."

"—I did."

He stopped short, looking over at me with wide eyes.

I nodded, slowly, the words falling from my lips like a waterfall of emotion that I'd buried deep.

"I always wanted to be with you. You were so kind and gentle and such a good friend. You were funny. You didn't treat me like Leo's sister, like everyone else. Even though Leo and I were the same age, it was always like I was just a kid or something. I guess I just didn't know how to tell you at the time."

"I can relate to that," he said. "I wasn't the best at expressing my emotions. I guess I never have been."

"You're doing pretty good right now," I said.

He smiled and Gracie brought our food and we dug in, eating in comfortable silence for a few minutes, the sound of the waves and the jingle of holiday songs filling in the gaps as we smiled across the table at each other.

I'd never been so happy to see someone in my life. And whatever the future held — tonight or a year from now — I was determined to do whatever it took to keep Wolfe close.

Now that I had him back, I didn't see any way I'd ever be able to say goodbye again.

CHAPTER 12

OLFE

DRIVING BACK to her house wrecked me.

Her words, her regrets, echoing in my mind as her body was pressed so close against mine, I could hardly breathe.

I had to remind myself she wasn't mine for the taking, no matter how either of us felt. Our first order of business was to find Leo and get him back to her safely. The fact that my body was begging to unleash my desire for her was my problem to deal with.

I pulled up to her house with steely reserve to do the right thing.

"I'll start another fire," she said, pulling off her helmet.

"Actually, I'm going to take off."

She looked at me in shock. "You are?"

"Yeah, I'm going to go find a hotel room. I saw The Whale Cove Inn had a vacant light on when we drove by."

"Oh," she said, the disappointment shining in her eyes. "Okay."

"I'll be back first thing in the morning, I promise. And I'm just a phone call away," I said, pulling her into my arms, and tempting my resolve. I made the hug brief and jumped back on the bike. She walked to the door slowly, looking back over her shoulder with a small smile before she opened the door and disappeared inside.

As soon as the door closed, I let out the breath I'd been holding in. I reached down to adjust my throbbing erection and started my bike back up and took off, my body on fire for her.

CHAPTER 13

ECEMBER

AFTER A RESTLESS NIGHT, there was a knock on my door at eight the next morning. I expected to see Wolfe standing there, but I opened it to find not just Wolfe, but three other terrifyingly large men with him.

My eyes widened, and I'm pretty sure my mouth dropped in surprise, but as soon as the three of them broke out into friendly smiles, I was immediately at ease.

Wolfe stood in front of them, holding up a white bag and a coffee cup.

"I thought you might need breakfast," he said. "Donuts?"

Those smiles were contagious. "Of course! Come in!" I said, moving out of the way. The other guys wore the same uniform Wolfe did - tight fitting jeans and leather jackets with the same Gods of Chaos patches on the back that Wolfe had.

"December, I'd like to introduce you to my friends. This is Wreck," he said, pointing at the smaller of the three, not that that meant he was small at all. Wreck was handsome, but he looked like he'd been through the wringer a few times. His skin was littered with scars, with a huge one cutting into his cheek, but the smile in his eyes as he shook my hand told me he was on the other side of whatever hell he'd been through.

"Happy to meet you," he said, nodding politely.

"And this is Storm," Wolfe said. Storm shook my hand and nodded, but sort of just grunted a greeting.

"Hi," I said, trying to drink them all in. There was a lot to drink.

"And this," Wolfe said, turning to the last of them, "is Slade."

Slade was the most interesting of the group, by far. His head was shaved and he had a spiky tattoo going up the side of his neck and trailing up onto his skull. His smile was wide and friendly and missing a tooth on the side. Bright blue and full of life, his eyes almost took my breath away.

"Hey, there, little mama," he said, a slight drawl to his voice, as he took my hand and instead of shaking it, kissed the back of my palm. His lips were warm and soft, a sharp contrast to his hand — which was rough and coarse and cold, his knuckles riddled with scars.

"Hello," I said, my insides quivering a little as I took my hand back. I was already insanely overwhelmed with Wolfe's presence, but now everything just went up a notch or two.

Wolfe sat the donuts and coffee down on the kitchen counter and walked over to me, placing a warm palm on the small of my back, instantly calming me.

"These are just a few of the Gods," he said. "Riot sent them down over night to help out."

"I see," I nodded, turning to them. "Thank you so much for coming."

"Hey, any opportunity to kick some ass is a pleasure," Slade said. My eyes widened at his words. I guess through all of this, I hadn't thought of any violence occurring, other than what I was trying to prevent — Shane hurting Leo.

Now that I had four very strong and scary men backing me up, talking about kicking ass, I felt a little uncomfortable, and yet empowered, at the same time. I've always had a problem with violence. Even avoiding things like boxing or wrestling or hunting.

Shane loved that stuff.

I wondered what he would think of these men standing in our living room — correction, my living room. Shane would never be welcomed back in this house. Not after all this bullshit. He'd given that privilege up the first time he laid a hand on Leo and myself.

I couldn't remember a time when Shane had been kind or affectionate or when we ever really exchanged any true, genuine love for each other. After Leo died, we were just going through the motions of raising our son and the rest just died away.

Now that Wolfe was here, waking up feelings inside of me that I thought were long gone, I realized just how much I'd been missing living with Shane all that time.

He was like an empty vessel, always trying to fill himself up with booze or accolades or who knows what else, and he certainly didn't have anything of value to give to me.

I was almost ashamed of myself for staying with him so long. I thought I was doing it for Leo, but these last few months have shown me that Leo didn't really need him either. He was thriving, actually, now that it was just the two of us at home and the anxiety of not knowing what kind of mood Shane would be in when he came back home wasn't there any more.

I missed him so much.

Leo's everything to me and if something happened to him, I know I wouldn't be able to go on.

Fortunately, with these behemoth dudes on my side, I had a lot more confidence that I was going to get my boy back.

I dug into the donuts and coffee, watching them carefully as they sauntered around my house.

"After you're done, we'll give Riot a call and figure out a plan of attack," Wolfe said. I nodded, my mouth full of donuts.

"Yeah, man, so it sounds like this baby daddy of yours is a real prick," Slade said. I almost choked on his words.

"That's definitely true," I replied, laughing.

"Wolfe told you about us?" he asked.

"He did," I said.

"Good. Don't you worry, mama. The Gods are gonna find that boy of yours."

Slade appeared to have full confidence and not a care in the world. In fact, they all did. I couldn't wait till Shane had to come face to face with them. The thought of him being put in his place, to have his ego knocked down a notch — after all these years — was almost orgasmic.

"And then what?" I asked.

"And then," Slade said, cracking his knuckles, laughing, "we kick ass!"

CHAPTER 14

HANE

"I DON'T KNOW why we're doing this in December anyway!"

Leo's complaints were getting to me. He was such a little pussy. I was so sick of his whining.

"You need to toughen up, boy!" I shouted. The wind whipped around the boat. The water was a little rocky today and I needed to pay a little more attention to things and his constant nagging wasn't helping.

"It's cold!" he insisted.

"You're wearing a coat!"

"It's not helping," he said, his voice cracking as if he were about to break out into tears.

"My god, Bud, it's not that bad," I said. "Grow some fucking balls!"

"The wind is about to knock us off the boat, and it's so cold, the rain is freezing! We can't even enjoy the view because of all the fog! How about you grow a brain, Dad?"

I snapped at his words. His blatant disrespect. The little shit was about to be a teenager — if I decided to let him live — and I knew if I didn't teach him not to disrespect me like that now, I never would be able to.

I didn't want to do it, but he'd left me no choice.

I slapped him. Hard. A hearty backhand across the face that sent him reeling across the other side of the boat. He looked at me like I'd killed his dumb dog or something.

"I hate you!" He flung his words at me like daggers, and it made me happy he knew how to get mad. Even if it was displaced anger flung my way. His stupid mother was always going on and on about love and happiness and kindness and being gentle — fuck that shit. You needed to access that anger in order to be a real man.

This boy was turning into a little pansy and if he wasn't going to toughen up on his own, I'd just have to do it myself. Maybe this trip was just what he needed. A chance to get away from December and all her soft, snowflake bullshit.

"You think I give a shit if you hate me? I'm not so fond of you myself, you little bastard!"

His eyes widened like I'd slapped him again and he ran away, disappearing down into the cabin with the dog following along behind him.

Just as well, I thought, as I flung open the storage area where I kept my booze. I cracked the seal on a new bottle of Makers and poured a good portion of it down my throat, its warmth shooting through me like little razors tearing through my guts.

It felt damned good.

I'd been going back and forth on whether I'd really kill the boy or not. I mean, he is my son. Maybe I could redeem him somehow, teach him better. I figured I'd give it a little more time and then I'd decide. But with the way he was acting, he wasn't doing himself any favors.

The more of a little bitch he was, the easier he was making it for me to decide.

CHAPTER 15

OLFE

HAVING the other guys there made it easier to keep my head on straight and my hands off December. Although, seeing Slade's slimy lips kissing her hand didn't help. I brushed it off and reminded myself that Slade was perfectly devoted to his wife Diana and I didn't have anything to worry about. He was just a relentless flirt and he couldn't help it.

Besides, it's not like I had any claim to her myself.

We'd all huddled around her kitchen island, Riot on the speakerphone as we listened in.

"Okay, so I did some digging. Shane did in fact buy a boat. December, if he was going to file a float plan with someone that would know to contact search and rescue if he didn't show up where he was expected, who would that be? Does he have a close friend or coworker?"

"Well, since it's not me, it's gotta be the Chief of the Lincoln County Sheriff's Department."

"That's what I thought, too. I'm going to try to hack into his email."

"You're going to hack into the Chief's email?" December asked, incredulously.

"Sure, it's not a big deal," Riot said. "If that doesn't work, then I'll try hacking into the Coast Guard's satellite systems and see if anyone has made contact with them."

"What should we do?" Slade asked.

"I've jumped the gun a little and just in case, I've rented you a boat of your own. It's probably a good idea to start preparing for a trip. Gods, go to the marina and pick up the keys and familiarize yourself. Storm, you know how to drive the boat, right?"

"I do," Storm replied. "My license is current, too."

"Great," he said. "December, can you concentrate on collecting some supplies? Food, drinks, anything the group of you might need for a few days' trip."

"Sure," December replied.

I looked over at Slade and noticed how quiet he was. He looked serious and a bit alarmed, which I'd never seen before.

"Okay, I'll be in touch real soon, once I have more information. Wolfe, I'm sending you the info for the boat rental on your phone right now."

"On it," I replied, hanging up the phone. I looked over at Slade. "What's going on with you?"

"Me?" he asked, surprised I'd noticed. "Man, look, I'm not a cage dude, but even more than that — I really fucking hate boats."

"Oh," I nodded. "You want to sit this one out, brother?"

"And lose the chance to kick someone's ass? No way, man. I'll be fine," he assured me. I was skeptical, but I let it go.

I turned to December and she was already rummaging around her kitchen and starting to pile groceries and supplies on her counter.

"I'll need to make a visit to the store," she said.

"That's fine," I said. "We can meet you at the marina."

"Sounds good," she said, smiling at me nervously. "Are you sure we won't get in trouble doing all this hacking?"

74

"Don't worry about it," I replied. "Riot's a pro and he won't do anything to put us in danger."

She nodded and squared her shoulders, putting on a brave face. Her courage was admirable and the fact that she wasn't breaking down was impressive. If it was my son that was missing, I wasn't sure I'd be able to remain so calm.

I hugged her quickly, letting her go before I could be overwhelmed by my own emotions, and we headed out.

All of Slade's talk about kicking ass had me riled up and Shane's face was front and center in my head, with a bright and shiny red target on it.

CHAPTER 16

ECEMBER

As I PUSHED the cart through the grocery store, it became heavier and heavier. I may have gone overboard but I had no experience in feeding four huge dudes, and I wasn't sure how long we'd be or if we'd be able to replenish our supplies easily, so I figured overdoing it was best.

By the time I got to check out, I could barely push the thing. I ignored the pointed looks from Charlene, the check-out girl that I'd gone to high school with.

When she started questioning me, I wasn't surprised.

"Having a party, December?" she asked.

"Not exactly," I said.

She squinted and looked at my cart with scrutiny.

"Well, whatever you're doing, whoever you're doing it for is most likely going to be bummed out by the lack of booze," she quipped. Charlene had a reputation for enjoying copious amounts of alcohol on a frequent basis, and I'd never been more thankful for it.

"You know what? You're right," I said, looking around. "Can you hold my order for a few minutes?"

She smacked her gum and laughed, her messy bun wiggling around on top of her head. "You betcha, doll."

I grabbed my now empty cart and pushed it quickly back to the beer aisle, loading it up with several cases of beer. When I got back to Charlene, her eyes widened with glee.

"Now, we've got a party!"

"I wish, girl, I wish," I said, shaking my head.

"Well, good luck, December, whatever's going on."

"Thanks," I said. I could have easily told her that Shane had taken Leo and me and a bunch of scary bikers were going out on a boat looking for them, but that sentence alone was so absurd I couldn't say it out loud.

Instead, I gave her a shaky smile and went out and loaded up my car, my body quivering with anticipation. I was struck by how much I'd relaxed since the Gods had arrived. I was impressed with their professionalism and efficiency, especially the man on the phone, Riot.

I thought back to how freaked out I was before I called Wolfe, how alone I'd felt, how alone I'd been. I'd been lost and had no idea where else to turn.

But as thankful as I was for them, I was still filled with worry for my son. It felt awful getting in my car all alone, which only emphasized the fact that Leo was gone.

I couldn't wait to be back in Wolfe's comforting presence again. He made this nightmare just a little easier to handle.

CHAPTER 17

OLFE

"Riot didn't spare any expense," Storm said, as we boarded the boat. Storm was right. It was huge. And luxurious.

We walked down to the cabin, and I was surprised to see it was divided into four small bedrooms with a large living and kitchen area in the middle.

"Apparently not," I said, whistling in approval. I was pleased to see how nice it was. In the back of my mind, I wanted to impress December, even though it wasn't my money renting this monster. But, I wanted her to be comfortable and confident in our ability to help her.

More than anything, I wanted to make sure Shane couldn't hurt her, or Leo, ever again. That rage was still boiling inside me, threatening to break to the surface at any moment. Luckily, many years behind bars had taught me how to control my emotions, so I was able to keep my anger at bay.

Storm was the only one of us with any boating experience, and he got to work familiarizing himself with all of the controls and operations.

"Let me know if you need help," I said.

"A baby like this will be a dream to operate," he said. "It practically does everything itself."

"Great," I said. I looked over at Slade and saw that he'd sat down on the couch, his knee bobbing up and down nervously.

"You good, man?" I asked.

"Yeah, yeah," he said, with a dismissive wave.

"There's still time to back out," I reminded him.

"Nope, I'm good," he said, standing up and climbing the stairs to the deck. Wreck and I followed him up, the snow still lightly falling around us. It was frigid and windy, not the best conditions for chasing someone up the coast. I silently cursed Shane for making all of us endure this shit.

The deck was slick and while the boat came with heavy parkas and life jackets for all of us to wear, the heavy leather boots we usually wore to ride our bikes weren't the best footwear when snow was falling steadily, sticking to the deck.

Slade slipped near the edge of the boat, almost tipping over the edge, but catching himself first.

"Dude!" I shouted. "Be fucking careful."

We were still anchored at the dock, waiting for December to arrive with our supplies, and the boat was barely swaying in the water but Slade already looked a little green.

"I'm fine," he said, putting a hand on his stomach. A slight sheen had formed on his upper lip.

"Are you sick?" I asked.

"No, just a little nauseous," he said. I shook my head, wondering how much worse he was going to get if we hadn't even started up the damned boat yet.

"Maybe you should go lay down," I said.

"Yeah, it's fucking windy as fuck out here," he said, disappearing below.

I turned to Wreck. "Wanna bet on how long it's going to be before he starts puking?"

Wreck laughed, shaking his head. "Sure, man. Five dollars says he's hugging the toilet in an hour tops."

"Probably right," I said. "I'll say two hours."

"Hopefully, we'll find this bastard before too long and can get back on solid ground."

"Nice pun," I said. "Solid Ground."

"Ah, right," he laughed. "So, you and December used to be a thing or what?"

"No, not really," I said, shrugging. "We kissed once. Many moons ago. Mostly, we were just friends. Her twin brother, Leo, was my best friend. I guess she was, too."

"What happened?"

"Leo died. December got pregnant. I went to prison for a crime I didn't commit. Not in that order, I guess."

"That's fucking rough, brother," he said. "It's obvious there's still something between the two of you, though."

"Why do you say that?"

"Just the way you look at each other. That's the kind of connection that never dies."

"Like the one between you and Frankie?"

"Exactly, dude. Hell, I thought Frankie was dead. And then, when she came back into my life, she had a whole new face and identity. I'd have never known it was her, except for the way I felt around her. It's like our bodies remembered each other. Even after all that time."

"I'm glad you found each other again," I said.

"If it wasn't for the Gods and Solid Ground, we wouldn't have."

"Thank the universe for the Gods, huh?"

"Fuck yeah," he said.

"Well, I don't know what's going to happen between me and December. I don't really think this is the right time to think about that stuff, either. We just gotta find Leo right now."

"Of course," Wreck replied, shrugging. "But I bet shit works out with y'all. I got a good feeling."

I paused, drinking in his words. "Me too," I said, softly. "Me too."

A honk from the parking lot caught our attention, and I saw December standing by her car and waving.

"A little help?" she called out.

We ran out to help her, making a couple of trips to bring in all the stuff she'd bought.

"I may have gone a little overboard," she said.

"With these guys, I doubt it will go to waste," I replied, as I brought several cases of beer on board. When Slade saw me bring it into the kitchen, he lunged for it.

"Oh, thank god," he said. "A fucking cure!"

"Sure about that?" Wreck asked. "Might make it worse."

"What's wrong?" December asked.

"Slade's got an aversion to boats."

"I'm fine!" he insisted, popping open a beer and taking a huge swig.

"This boat is amazing," December said. "It must go really fast, huh?"

Her eyes were full of hope, laced with worry, and I wanted to pull her into my arms and tell her everything was going to be okay. Instead, I kept my hands to myself and flashed her what was hopefully a reassuring smile.

"It does go fast," I said. "And Storm really seems to know what he's doing. You'll have your boy back in your arms in no time."

"I hope you're right. Any word from Riot?"

"He called a few minutes ago. Turns out, Shane emailed his boss a float plan. That doesn't mean he's going to stick to it, but it's a start."

"Wow, I can't believe Riot was able to find it."

"Believe it," I said. "Riot is a genius."

"That's so great, where did Shane say they were going?"

"North. Their destination was listed as somewhere near the Strait of Juan de Fuca."

"That far? That's almost to Canada."

"I know," I replied. "But hopefully, he won't get that far."

"All good down there? Ready to take off?" Storm called down into the cabin.

"Sure, man, you need help with anything?" I asked.

"Yeah, I could use an extra pair of hands with the lines for a minute," he replied.

Wreck stood up and walked up on deck, "I got it."

December started putting everything away as the sound of the boat's engine roaring to life vibrated through the vessel. Within seconds, we were in motion, the boat jolting forward and quickly picking up speed. I joined December in putting away the groceries, our bodies brushing against each other in the small kitchen, sending the fire raging inside of me.

I'd always been attracted to her. I'd lain awake in my cell for years remembering the curves of her hips, the way she smiled, my body yearning for her. And now that we were together again, all these years later, it was more intense than it had ever been.

She smiled up at me and it took all my strength not to wrap my arms around her and kiss her the way I wanted to.

Fuck it, I thought, finally. I'd waited so long. Why wait any longer?

Throwing all caution to the wind, I grabbed her arms and looked into her eyes, my head bending down towards her.

I needed to feel her mouth on mine.

I needed to taste her, to kiss her…

Suddenly, Slade jumped up and ran to the bathroom, the sound of his violent retching echoing through the cabin, ruining any chance of me actually getting to kiss her and costing me five bucks all at the same time.

CHAPTER 18

ECEMBER

As soon as the boat took off, a surge of adrenaline rushed through my veins. It felt good to be moving, to finally do something to try to find Leo.

For a second, I'd thought Wolfe was going to kiss me in the kitchen, but Slade interrupted us and the moment was over in a flash.

Wolfe and I walked up on deck once everything was put away, standing at the edge of the boat and watching the Christmas lights on the marina disappear as we moved farther away.

"It doesn't feel like much of a Christmas at all," I sighed.

"It will," Wolfe said. "As soon as you and Leo are back home, safe and sound, everything will get back to normal."

"I hope not," I said. "I don't want normal. Normal was always worrying about Shane and what kind of hell he was going to be bringing home next. I never want him in our lives again."

Wolfe nodded, and I knew he was holding back. He had every right in the world to hate Shane, just as much as me, if not more.

"You can say whatever you want," I urged.

"I'm not much of a talker," he said, his voice gruff. Wind whipped my hair around my head, biting my cheeks with its frigid caress.

"Well, you must have an opinion about Shane."

"I've never liked Shane, I'll admit that," he said. "Not before that night, and not after. I didn't confess because I liked Shane. I don't think that's ever been a secret."

"Why didn't you like him before?" I asked, turning my face up to him.

He stared down at me for a moment before replying.

"Because he was fucking arrogant. And selfish," he paused, before going on, "and because he got you."

"Me?"

"Yes, December. You."

"Oh," I nodded, my heart in my throat, words failing me. I wanted to fall into his arms and pretend this nightmare wasn't really happening, but I couldn't stop thinking about Leo.

"Sail onnnn, honey, good times, never felt soooo gooooood," Slade began singing at the top of his lungs, the beer obviously coursing through his veins now. "Sail onnnnn, sugarrrr, good times, never felt sooo goooood."

"Oh, my god," I giggled, the mood lightened. Wolfe laughed along with me.

"You must be feeling better, brother," Wolfe said.

"A little," he said. "I miss Diana, though."

"Who's Diana?"

"Diana is only the prettiest little filly this side of the Mississippi," Slade replied, his voice slurred. "And also the mother of my lovely son, and my darling partner."

"Oh," I said. "She must be very special to be with a man like you."

"Indeed she is!" he shouted, his words carried away by the wind as he broke out into song again. "Hey, y'all, sing with me! Well, it's not far down from paradise, at least it's not for me, and if the wind is right you can sail away, find tranquility..."

I rolled my eyes and turned to Wolfe. "Dinner?"

"Sounds good," he laughed.

"I'll cook, maybe you should keep an eye on your drunken sailor," I said.

"Will do," Wolfe said, winking.

I headed downstairs, my heart swelling with happiness that Wolfe seemed to have found a tribe of his own. The family we'd formed together so long ago had been blasted to smithereens and I was so glad to know that he'd found others to bond with after he was freed.

He was a good man, who'd surrounded himself with other good men, and I was thankful for that.

Maybe I'd not ruined his life completely after all.

A sense of relief washed over me and a little bit of regret fell away. I didn't know if there was a future for us, but at least I knew Wolfe would be okay, no matter what.

And that was enough.

CHAPTER 19

EO

LOOKING out into the night sky, it felt peaceful, for the first time since we'd left. Once it started getting dark, Dad anchored about a mile offshore, and now that he was asleep, and all was quiet and still, I was amazed at how beautiful it was.

Dad said we came on this trip to bond, but it was obvious he wasn't interested in that. From his conversation I'd overheard, I knew that was a lie. He was only doing this to piss off my mother.

It was cruel.

But I wasn't surprised. Dad never seemed to do anything to make her happy. I was convinced they didn't love each other, and I wasn't sure why they were ever together.

I guess it was because of me.

But that didn't make me feel any better.

In fact, it made me feel worse.

I just wanted to get home with Lucy and have this whole thing be over, but I didn't even know how long it would be before we turned around. Dad said we were going 'up to the Strait', but all I knew was that it was near the Canadian border and he wouldn't tell me his plans after that.

I snuck into the wheelhouse and spotted the radio, grabbing it and saying a little prayer that we were close enough to shore for me to call for help. Dad would be pissed, but I didn't care.

None of this felt right to me and I just wanted to go home.

It didn't matter, though, because all I got was static.

"Hello?" I whispered, pressing the button, waiting, hoping for a voice to answer me.

I tried again, a few more times, but all I got was static and silence.

I placed the radio back in its holder with a sigh and headed out to the deck. Dad kept his cell phone in his pocket while he slept, so even if it had reception, it probably wouldn't work this far out.

I stared up at the endless stars, sparkling in the deep black sky, the moon hanging bright off in the distance.

I couldn't help but worry about my mother. She must be worried sick herself. It just wasn't fair.

I thought back on the day and how awful it was. Dad only seemed interested in drinking and yelling at me. Maybe they went hand in hand, but I wouldn't know because all he did was drink these days. I couldn't even remember how he was when he wasn't drinking.

I spotted his cooler in the corner and walked over and opened it. It was full of beer and half empty bottles of liquor. With a smile, I grabbed each bottle, one by one, and poured the contents out over the side of the boat, the amber liquid sparkling in the moonlight. By the time I was done, there was one beer left and a bunch of empty bottles.

I put them in the recycling bin and Lucy and I headed back to bed.

Maybe tomorrow would be better now.

CHAPTER 20

ECEMBER

AFTER ANCHORING for the night so Storm could rest a few hours, we had dinner and divided up the space so we could all crash.

The boat had three small bedrooms and a bigger master bedroom that the guys insisted I take, but I hated the thought of sleeping alone. As I was washing my face and brushing my teeth, I wondered what Wolfe would say if I asked him to sleep with me.

Was it wrong?

I wanted so much from him, so much that I really couldn't even think about right now, but mostly, I just needed to be held. The pain and worry about Leo had exhausted me and as grateful as I was to have the help of these amazing men, I still felt alone and sad.

Wolfe had stayed close to me all day and I wasn't ready to let that go.

I decided I'd ask. The worst he could do was say no.

Slade, Wreck and Storm had already gone to bed and I found Wolfe in the kitchen drinking a beer.

"Hey there," I whispered, not wanting to wake up anyone else. The boat swayed gently, as if it wanted to rock us all to sleep.

"Hey," he whispered back. "Ready for bed?"

"I guess," I said.

"I know it's hard to stop for the night, but we'll make good time tomorrow."

"I know," I replied. "The hard part is sleeping alone. Will you sleep with me?"

I blurted the words out and instantly regretted it. His eyes widened and I tried to take them back.

"Nevermind, I shouldn't have —."

"December."

"Yes?"

"Of course, I will sleep with you. I know how hard this is. I'd do anything you asked of me."

"Anything?" I asked, bemused.

He grew serious, his eyes peering deeply into mine. I saw the desire there, and I felt it, too, but making love to Wolfe for the first time on a boat with a bunch of other guys wasn't how I'd imagined it.

And, oh, how I'd imagined it over the years.

By the look in Wolfe's eyes, I was sure he'd imagined it too.

"Thank you," I whispered. I turned and headed down the small hall towards my bedroom and I felt his eyes on my back as he followed.

I couldn't help but smile. All I wanted was to be wrapped up in Wolfe's arms, relish in the comfort he provided, and his agreement left me breathless.

I kept my clothes on and crawled into bed, scrambling under the covers. Respectfully, almost too much so, Wolfe stayed on top of the covers as he pulled me into his arms, wrapping me up in the comfort I so desperately needed.

Words unnecessary, we lay together in the silence of the swaying boat, our breath falling in sync as we drifted off to sleep, exhaustion settling in as the light from the full moon poured through the window and bathed us in her glowing light.

CHAPTER 21

HANE

THE BRIGHT MORNING sunlight shot through my brain, sending searing jolts of torturous agony through my head. I groaned, stumbling to the bathroom.

When I came out, Leo was on the deck, staring out at the water with Lucy sitting by his feet.

"Morning," I grumbled.

"Hey," he mumbled.

Lovely. *Another day with this asshole,* I thought to myself. He was so ungrateful. Not a humble damned bone in his body. All he did was sit around and sulk, and he never thanked me once for bringing his sorry ass into this world.

I thought back to the moment December told me she was pregnant. I was already scared out of my fucking mind that Wolfe would change his mind and tell the truth about what happened that night at the convenience store.

Not that he knew the real truth, anyway, but if he told anyone I was there, his confession would be useless and they'd come after me in a heartbeat.

It had been a few weeks since it all went down and I'd considered going to try to visit Wolfe while he was still in County but I figured staying as far away from that scene as possible was the best thing for me.

We were never close in the first place, so going to visit him would only stir up suspicions. But, for that few weeks after it all happened and before December dropped the baby bomb on my ass, I'd been planning my escape.

I didn't want to leave too soon, for the same reason I didn't visit Wolfe. I didn't want to seem like I was doing anything unusual. So, I was waiting for the right time, but I'd been socking away as much money as I could and figuring out where the hell I could go and start over.

There was nothing to keep me in Depoe Bay.

Certainly not December. All she did was cry and cry, going on and fucking on about losing Leo. Goddamn, she was almost catatonic. It was maddening and I was quickly growing bored of it all.

Leaving was looking better and better everyday.

Until she decided to throw a wrench into things.

"I'm pregnant, Shane," she'd finally confessed through tears. "I don't know what to do."

Well, fuck.

Everything changed after that. I tried to get her to get rid of the kid, adoption, abortion, whatever, hell, I didn't care. To be perfectly honest, I thought about doing something myself to help it all along.

But I'd already tempted fate and I didn't need another death on my hands.

So, out of guilt, I stayed.

Goddamn, I wish I'd bailed.

But one thing led to another and I ended up being a cop, so I guess life works out the way it's supposed to, in the end. Of course, I couldn't have the kind of freedom I'd always dreamed of, not saddled with a fucking kid and an old lady.

But I did my best, I guess. I had a good time, to the best of my ability.

But now? Now that the brat was about to turn into a full on teenager, with the entitled attitude to go along with it?

No, thank you.

I was ready for this whole shit show to be over with.

I knew the only remedy for the relentless throbbing in my head was the hair of the dog that bit me, so I sauntered over to my cooler for my morning medicine. Alcohol had been my only friend through all this shit. It blurred the edges of reality just enough to make it tolerable.

I threw open the lid and stared down at the empty cooler in confusion. Next to it was a crate I'd been throwing my empties in, and it was filled with empty bottles. Beer bottles, and my liquor bottles, all completely empty.

"What the fuck?" I mumbled under my breath, attempting to remember just how much I'd drank the night before. It was fuzzy, super fuzzy. And my head did feel like a Mac truck was running through it. I looked over at the boy, my eyes squinted in suspicion.

Did he have the balls to drink my stash?

No way. I shook my head. He didn't have that kind of courage. He'd have known what kind of hell he would be unleashing on himself and he'd never do that.

Luckily, we were still anchored only about a mile offshore, so replenishing my stock wouldn't be too much of a chore.

I walked over to him, sizing him up as I went along.

He didn't look drunk. Or hungover. I was still doubting whether he'd done it or not, but I figured it was important to address the situation, no matter what.

"You drink my booze?"

He looked up at me, his eyes, so much like December's, defiant and angry.

"Why would I drink that shit? It's disgusting."

I lifted an eyebrow at his language. Maybe he was getting a little hair on his sack after all.

"All my shit is gone, every last drop."

"Yeah? Maybe you drank it. Which makes you disgusting, too."

The back of my hand was slamming into his face before I even had time to think about it, sending him flying from his chair. Lucy jumped, then growled at me, jumping between us like I wouldn't hit her, too.

Dogs are so fucking stupid.

Leo looked up at me with hatred in his eyes. I stared back at him, reflecting the disdain we had for each other like we were looking in a mirror.

"I fucking hate you!" he shouted at the top of his lungs, before scrambling to his feet and running down to the cabin.

I laughed, shaking my head, as I began to pull up the anchor and head towards the shore to find more booze.

CHAPTER 22

OLFE

DECEMBER FELL asleep right away and I laid awake all night.

She snuggled in my arms like a long-lost lover and yet we still hadn't kissed. I wasn't counting the one when we were kids, because did that really count at all? No. What counted was the present, and that meant we were starting from scratch. But somehow, even that thought didn't feel right.

But December? Lying in my arms all night? The feel of her heartbeat linking up with mine, as if they'd been connected all these years in some fateful way?

Yeah, that felt right as rain.

At some point, after the sun rose over the horizon, I finally fell asleep despite my best efforts to stay awake. I had no idea what dawn might bring with it, and I'd learned a long time ago not to take anything for granted. This might be my only opportunity to hold December like that. I didn't want to miss a second.

My body finally betrayed me, though, and I did fall asleep fast and hard — so hard that I had a familiar dream. When I woke up, I was hard and hot and throbbing and I knew if I didn't untangle myself from December's still slumbering body — then I would either make a complete fool of myself or peel those sheets back and find out if what I'd been dreaming of all these years lived up to my imagination.

So, I left her there, hating myself for being so weak in the moment. I went to the bathroom and ripped off my clothes, turning on the icy water and immersing myself.

It was no use.

My body wasn't going to take no for an answer, so I had to find my own relief, my eyes closed as I relived my delicious dream, my hands sliding over December's hips, gripping them firmly as I slammed myself inside of her warmth. I shuddered in pleasure, finally finding the empty substitute that would have to suffice for sustenance.

At least for now.

A small glimmer of hope had found its way into my boarded up heart somewhere between when December fell asleep in my arms last night and when I woke up from dreaming I was literally inside of her.

Instead, she'd gotten inside of me.

Hell, she always was.

No matter what happened today, as we were getting closer and closer to finding Shane and Leo, I knew nothing in the world would ever change that.

What happened in the future was still unknown, but that hope that had taken residence deep inside of me was high.

I pulled on my jeans after drying off, and avoided December's bedroom all together, joining the guys in the kitchen.

It was obvious I'd spent the night in December's bed, but I wasn't trying to hide anything, either. The look Slade gave me as I walked in the room did not go unnoticed, but I didn't acknowledge it either.

Luckily, he kept his mouth shut, which wasn't like him at all, which actually worried me.

"You okay, man?" I asked.

"Yeah, yeah," he said. "Feeling much better."

"That's good," I said.

He shook his head, "I mean, I don't think I'm as good as you, though, brother," he smirked, gesturing toward December's room.

"There it is," I said. "I thought we'd get through the morning without your snide comments."

"Never, man," he said, laughing as the other others joined in. "I'll never be that fucking sick."

CHAPTER 23

ECEMBER

AFTER CHANGING CLOTHES, I walked out of my room and stopped short when I saw the guys in the kitchen laughing. They were all gorgeously stunning men, but it was Wolfe that left me reeling.

He stood with his back to me, half-naked in just a pair of jeans. He turned when I walked in and the laughter faded away, as I stood staring at him in awe.

I hadn't seen Wolfe's half-naked body since he was a boy when we were swimming and even then I couldn't help but stare. But now, all traces of the boy I knew were gone and the man standing in front of me had my mouth watering.

"Hey," he said, flashing me a smile.

"Good morning," I replied, forcing myself to look away.

"Hungry? The guys made breakfast," he said. "Storm's upstairs and we pulled anchor hours ago."

"Good, yeah, I'm hungry," I said.

I walked over and grabbed a plate, as Slade moved out of the way and flashed me a friendly smile. "Morning, mama."

"Good morning," I replied. "Are you feeling better?"

"Absolutely, totally ready for a kick-ass day!"

"Isn't everyday a kick ass day for you, Slade?" Wreck asked, laughing.

"If it's a good day, then that means I kicked some ass, you fucking bet!" Slade replied, walking over to Wreck and throwing his fists up. "Let's fucking fight, bro!"

"Not on the boat!" Wolfe said, shaking his head. "You goddamned maniac."

Slade put his hands down, shaking his head with disappointment. Wolfe looked over at me and smiled. "He loves to fight."

"I gathered that," I said, not able to do anything but laugh along with them.

"Well, today's the fucking day, I can feel it in my bones," Slade said. "Can't wait to break a few bones myself."

"Let's wait till we've accomplished our mission," Wolfe said.

"Or, maybe during the mission? I mean, that's the fun of it all, isn't it?"

Wolfe's phone rang and he walked out onto the deck, leaving me there to sit with the guys at the small bar and eat my breakfast. Slade kept trying to dance around Wreck, begging him to fight. It was entertaining and I was happy to watch.

The look on Wolfe's face when he returned alarmed me, wiping away any trace of a smile on my face.

"What's wrong?"

"Fuck," he said, shaking his head as he ran a hand through his hair.

"What's up, dude? Spill it," Slade said.

"That was Riot," he said. "He got a hit on the boat's GPS but it was last night. He checked again this morning and it's been disabled."

"Disabled?" I asked. "So that means we don't know where they are."

"That's exactly what that means," he replied. "All we have to go on now is the float plan and there's no guarantee he's going to follow that."

I nodded, my heart sinking, tears springing to my eyes.

I jumped up and ran to the bedroom, slamming the door and flinging myself on the bed as huge sobs of disappointment washed over me.

CHAPTER 24

EO

MY PLAN HADN'T GONE as well as I'd hoped.

I thought maybe if he wasn't drunk, Dad would be okay to be around. I was wrong. It was obvious he didn't care about me. He only cared about his booze and whatever sick revenge he thought he was getting on Mom.

My eye swelled quickly and it throbbed painfully. Lucy stayed extra close to me now, but her little body was shivering with fear.

For the first time, I realized how much I hated my father. I wished he wasn't my father, that I had someone normal to look up, someone who was kind and gentle and protective and loving.

Not whatever he was.

He was a monster and I wanted to get as far away from him as possible. Unfortunately, the boat didn't allow that. I was almost grateful when we drifted into a small marina in Astoria. I jumped off the boat before he could even drop the anchor, anxious to get away, if even for a moment.

There was a little store for the boaters right near the marina, as well as a place to gas up. As Dad filled the tank, I took Lucy and let her pee outside, then tied her up and went inside and looked around, gathering a bunch of chips and candy and soda to take back on the boat. I was the only one in the store, and I could feel the man behind the counter staring at me.

When I dumped all the stuff on the counter, he lifted a brow.

"My Dad will be in to pay in a minute," I said, turning away.

"Son?" His voice was warm and kind, and hearing him say that word, without it being laced with anger, threw me a little. I turned to see his eyes full of concern. "Are you alright, son? Do you need some help?"

He pointed at my eye and I realized I'd almost forgotten about it. I reached up, touching it gingerly, hesitating. Should I ask for help? Could he help me? Maybe he could hide me and call my Mom and I could wait somewhere for her. My head started spinning with possibilities, and I opened my mouth, the words forming in my head before making it to my lips.

The door opened and Dad walked in, my mouth slamming shut before I could say anything at all. The man looked over at Dad then back at me, his eyes squinting suspiciously.

"Did you get your shit?" Dad growled my way.

"Yeah," I mumbled, avoiding the man's eye.

Dad pulled three cases of beer out of the cooler and dropped them on the counter next to my snacks, then scanned the shelves behind the clerk.

"I'll take a bottle of Maker's — no, make that two — and a bottle of Patron. The biggest one you have."

The man turned to pull the bottles from the shelves, turning back to face Dad.

"That it?" he asked.

"I filled my tank outside," he said.

The man nodded, hitting the buttons on his register, and taking Dad's money. All the while, he was stealing glances at me, but I couldn't look at him again. If Dad knew I was about to try to make a run for it, he'd hurt me even more.

"Carry your shit!" Dad growled angrily. I shuffled over and grabbed the bag the man had filled and walked out the door, Dad following along behind me after I untied Lucy, cussing at me for going too slow as we walked back to the boat, my heart filled with dread at having to get back on there and be alone with him again.

CHAPTER 25

ECEMBER

I DIDN'T WANT to break down in front of everyone. I'd kept it together so well so far, but knowing we couldn't track them now had dashed every ounce of hope I had.

A few minutes after running out, Wolfe softly knocked on my door.

"Hey, can I come in?" he asked. He was so kind and polite, it almost broke my heart.

"Yeah," I said, wiping my eyes and trying to pull it together. But as soon as he sat down on the bed and pulled me into his arms, I lost it again.

"Shhh, it's okay, babe," he said, holding me tightly. His warm palm caressed my hair as I rested my head on his shoulder. "We're going to find him. Trust us. Riot knows what he's doing, I promise. He has some other tricks up his sleeve. It's just going to take a little time."

"What if it's too late?" I daringly uttered the words that had been banging around my head for days.

"It's not."

"What if it is?" I said, pulling away and searching his eyes.

He took a deep breath, shaking his head.

"Do you really want me to answer that, December?"

"Yes," I said, stubbornly.

"Fine," he said. "If it's too late and Shane's hurt even one hair on Leo's head, I will rip him apart with my bare hands."

It felt good to hear that. It was what I was thinking myself. I was furious with Shane, ready to kill him myself, if necessary.

"Okay," I nodded. "We'll kill him together."

"No," he said, shaking his head. "This kind of thing is our job. It's what we do. I'm not about to put you in any danger, December. You're going to have to let me — and the Gods — handle this."

I didn't want to argue with him.

I didn't have the strength.

His words were meant to comfort me, and while they did that, they did something else, too. I wanted so badly to believe him, to trust him — to rely on him.

Since Wolfe had walked back into my life — since I'd pulled him back into my nightmare, that is — he'd done nothing but be a rock that I could lean on. Without hesitation, he'd come running when I needed him.

He was the man I should have been with all these years.

He should have been Leo's father.

He should have been the man I built a life with, not the lunatic I'd ended up with. His arms were still wrapped around me, his massively thick arms bound around me like a shield from any pain the world might heap upon me.

I wished like hell they'd been there all along.

My eyes searched his, looking for the answer to a question I'd never asked.

"Wolfe," I whispered his name when I saw the answer I'd always needed in his eyes. I glanced at his lips, then back up into his fiery eyes.

His lips crashed into mine and the whole world stopped.

Years of pent up emotion exploded inside of me, the heat of his kiss igniting the fire I'd spent so long trying to extinguish.

He kissed me with an intense passion and I matched it, needing every sensation coursing through me, years of yearning rushing to the surface and begging for release.

Our kiss lingered, his tongue parting my lips and slipping inside. I opened my mouth, welcoming him into my heart where he'd always had a home.

CHAPTER 26

OLFE

She tasted like heaven.

Like the gates of heaven had opened up just for me, and I'd been invited in to taste the celestial ambrosia I'd always dreamed of.

Our tongues tangled together, our mouths searching deeply for the connection we'd both tried to ignore. My hands caressed her back, pulling her closer, needing her body pressed against mine before I went absolutely crazy with desire for her.

My breath seemed to stop, as well as my heart, as I kissed her with all the passion my body possessed.

I wanted to chase all her demons away, put the light back in her heart before everything went black.

I wanted to love her like I should have been loving her ever since I'd first kissed her all those years ago.

Just as she began to melt into my arms, our bodies sliding back onto the bed, our hands exploring the flesh we'd hungered for for so long, my phone buzzed in my pocket.

With a painful groan, I wrenched my arms from around her and pulled it out of my pocket.

"It's Riot," I said, sitting up.

"Brother," I answered. "What's up?"

"I've been listening in on the scanners in the coastal towns," he said. "A man in a marina convenience store in Astoria called the cops and reported a man and an older boy that seemed suspicious."

"You think it's them?" I asked.

"It could be," he said. "Is December with you?"

"Yeah," I answered.

"Well, maybe keep this part to yourself, but the man said the boy didn't look good. He had a swollen and bruised eye and it was like he was trying to ask for help."

"I see," I said, my head trying to quickly analyze how much I should tell December. Riot was right to protect her. But lying to her felt so wrong.

"Did they get back on the boat?"

"Yeah, he said they were headed north."

"Towards the Strait," I said.

"In that general direction, yes," Riot said. "I think you're on the right track. Stay the course and keep going. The cops said they were calling the Coast Guard to ask them to investigate and look for the boat."

"Oh yeah? Well, that's more than the assholes in Lincoln County did."

"Well, Shane's not one of their men they need to protect, so maybe we'll get lucky here."

"Thanks, man," I said. "I'll tell the others and tell Storm to pick up the pace a little."

"Yep," Riot said. "Everything good there?"

"Yeah, man, sure," I replied. "Slade was a little sick yesterday, but I think he's a little better today."

"He fucking hates boats," Riot laughed. "That's why I sent him with you. He's always fucking with me, I gotta get my punches in when I can."

"Well, score one for you, brother, he was practically green yesterday."

Riot laughed, "I'll be in touch soon. Give Slade my love."

"Will do," I said, hanging up the phone.

"What!?" December asked. She was sitting next to me, her eyes wide.

I took a deep breath.

There was no way in hell I could tell this woman a lie.

CHAPTER 27

HANE

WHEN I LEFT Depoe Bay with Leo, I only had a loose plan in place. Now that I was becoming more frustrated with him, and the further we got away from that god awful town, my plan began to come more into focus.

I spent most of the day sitting out on the deck, bundled up against the wind, a never-ending glass of whiskey in my hand, and my head full of fantasizing about what it would feel like to be free.

I fucking hated being a cop, almost as much as I hated being a father.

The idea of starting over fresh somewhere was extremely appealing. I'd have to assume a new identity, of course. Maybe it was best if Shane died with Leo. Then, both of us would be free and I could start over as an entirely new person, somewhere up north.

I'd visited the islands around the Strait once when I was a kid with my folks, and I'd never forgotten how beautiful it was. A ninety-six-mile body of water that leads from the Salish Sea to the Pacific Ocean, it feels like another world completely. Hundreds of small cabins are sprinkled along its shores, and the thought of finding one of them to disappear into sounded like heaven.

Nobody to tell me what to do.

Nobody to remind me of all the mistakes I've made.

No more having to see Leo's face — which looked so much like his dead uncle's face — a constant reminder of that fucked up night. I was so far beyond blaming myself. In my mind, all that shit went sour because of Leo. If he'd only kept his cool, he might still be alive.

Instead, I was stuck living in a prison of responsibilities that I never fucking asked for.

It just wasn't fucking fair. I deserved better than this boring life.

I walked down into the cabin, ignoring Leo and Lucy lying in bed together, his nose in a book, like most days. It was obvious all of my feelings were mutual, because he didn't even look up.

I opened the closet and pulled out my backpack, unzipping it and pulling my handgun out.

I was close to putting my plan in place. I just needed to think a few more details through. But when I was ready, I wanted to be ready right there in that second, so I didn't have time to change my mind.

With my gun in hand, I headed back upstairs, my head spinning a mile a minute.

CHAPTER 28

EO

WE DIDN'T SPEAK to each other the entire day.

Instead, Dad poured the booze down his throat all day, speeding through the water like a madman. At times, I could hear him out there, seemingly cussing the wind. The snow had finally stopped, but the wind was so sharp and biting that I stayed down in the cabin, enjoying the heat and the protection from the relentless wind.

Dad drove for a while, even after it got dark, but he finally dropped anchor and drank himself to sleep.

I was starting to like the evenings alone. I could breathe a little easier as he slept and I wandered upstairs to look out at the stars. Now that we weren't moving, the wind wasn't as brutal. I sat down in Dad's chair, looking up at the sparkling, black sky, plagued with endless worry for Mom.

I wondered if she was looking for me. *But who would help her?* I hated that she was all alone. I wondered if the cops Dad worked with would help her, but from the sound of Dad's conversation with his boss, I figured not.

I tiptoed downstairs and found Dad's cell phone had slipped out of his pocket and was on the floor. I grabbed it quietly and took it back upstairs.

As I suspected, there was no service. Nothing. We were too far from shore again.

I sighed, flipping through the pictures on his phone out of boredom. His gallery didn't hold even one picture of me or Mom and it made me sad. Maybe he'd never loved me. Maybe he never would.

I pulled up his email and saw a bunch of messages from Mom. I opened one and began reading, my heart racing in my chest. She was begging him to come home, to bring me home. I scrolled down, hating that she was so scared.

When I saw the message he'd sent her first, I froze.

"Consider Leo lost at sea..."

What did that mean? My thoughts drifted to this afternoon when Dad pulled his gun from the closet. I never thought for a second it was for me. Dad always liked to have his gun close, so I just figured it was some weird ego thing.

Did he plan to kill me?

Tears stung my eyes and I felt like I couldn't breathe. I tried to type out a message to Mom, but every time I hit send, it wouldn't go through.

Frantically, I threw the phone down and began pacing, Lucy's alarmed gaze tracking my every movement.

I had to think.

I had to get away.

I had to stay alive.

Lucy jumped up suddenly and ran to the stern and I followed her. When I saw the blinking of another boat's bright red lights in the distance, I almost shouted in joy.

I began jumping up and down, waving my arms as it neared. Lucy danced at my feet, sensing my excitement. I kept waving, unsure if they could even see me in the dark. I ran into the wheelhouse and began turning our own lights on and off, before running back out and waving again.

When I saw them turn on a bright spotlight and shine it my way, my heart skipped a beat. As they came closer, the blue logo on the side of their boat told me it was the Coast Guard.

"Help!" I called out, waving to the man who'd appeared on their bow. "Help! Help!"

Lucy chimed in, barking at the quickly approaching boat.

My Mom's face flashed in my head and I could see her smile. She was going to be so happy to have me home. I couldn't wait to hug her.

Tears of happiness sprang to my eyes as the smile of the officer came into view.

CHAPTER 29

HANE

THE BOY'S screams woke me up.

"What the fuck?" I roared, my head spinning as I jumped to my feet way too fast. The room spun as I grabbed my gun and stumbled up to the deck. I turned the corner and saw Leo waving and jumping as a Coast Guard boat approached, the boat's spotlight shining brightly on us.

If they knew how wasted I was, they'd arrest me.

I could try to talk my way out of it, but the Coast Guard was infamous for not being too fond of actual police officers. We were not on the same side.

And Leo's black eye wasn't going to do me any favors.

In an instant, the future I'd been dreaming of disappeared before my eyes and my hopefulness was replaced by white-hot anger.

How dare Leo ruin this for me too!

I raised my gun, my finger squeezing the trigger.

CHAPTER 30

ECEMBER

"I KNOW it doesn't sound great, but it means he's alive, December."

Wolfe was doing his best to comfort me, but my anger at Shane was raging through my veins. A black eye? My sweet boy?

I wanted to kill Shane, there's no denying my feelings.

But Wolfe was right. Leo was alive, and that's what mattered. And, if it was really them, then we were on the right track and maybe we'd get to him soon. I had no idea how much time we were making, but the boat seemed to be working overtime as we sped through the water.

I'd never been more grateful for a bunch of burly dudes in my life.

"It's going to be dark soon," I said.

"That's true," Storm said. We were all sitting on the deck near the wheelhouse, trying to make conversation to pass the time. "But I showed Wreck how to operate the boat and we won't need to stop for the night. He can drive while I catch a little sleep. We should be gaining on them."

"That's awesome," I said, looking over at Wreck. "Thank you."

"My pleasure, December," he said. They'd all been so polite and kind, all of them giving me the space I needed as I lived through this bullshit nightmare. Except for Wolfe, and to be perfectly honest, I wanted even less space between us.

That glimmer of hope was back, shining through my heart like a bright light that I couldn't turn out, even if I wanted to.

My thoughts turned to the future, once I had Leo back in my arms and was done with Shane for good. I vowed to keep Leo away from Shane, if it was the last thing I did.

But what about once all this was over?

What did that mean for me and Wolfe? His kisses had left me breathless, and I was anxious to kiss him again. Once Riot's call interrupted us, though, we'd run upstairs to tell the others the news, and we'd been up here ever since, but I wasn't oblivious to the glances he kept throwing my way, his eyes full of a secret pleasure that must have matched my own.

After a while, Slade and Storm went down to sleep and Wreck took the wheel, leaving Wolfe and I alone on deck. He reached over and grabbed my hand, turning it over to place a searing kiss on my palm that took my breath away.

My eyes crashed into his, and the dark hunger I saw there made me gasp.

The future was uncertain, to say the least. I didn't know if Wolfe would stick around after we got Leo back. *Who could blame him if he didn't?* We were a constant reminder of everything he'd lost. And he had an important job.

Where did all that leave me? Where did it leave *us?*

The harsh reality of our situation is that all we had was right here, right now and I had lived my life as one big, missed opportunity and I wasn't about to give up this one, too.

I turned my palm back over, grabbing his hand and pulling him to his feet. Without a word, I guided him back downstairs to my bedroom and closed the door behind us.

I turned back to him, staring up at him, my eyes searching his.

"Wolfe, make love to me."

His mouth opened in surprise, but in a flash, his mouth crashed into mine in the most delicious collision of the past and the present, the missed love of forgotten years mingling with the possibilities of our present, our bodies relishing in the opportunity to finally right our destinies that had gone so horribly wrong.

His heat poured into me, love and desire and pain and pleasure melting together into a profound mixture of pure, raw emotion.

He tore away from me, his eyes dark and stormy, the boat slightly swaying under our feet.

"December, I've waited all my life to show you how I feel about you," he growled, his voice low and thick.

"Me, too," I whispered, tears filling my eyes.

"I love you," he said, his arms wrapping around me. "I've always loved you."

"I love you, too, Wolfe, so much," I said. "I've loved you forever."

"Forever," he said, a smile stretching across his face. "Are you sure you want to do this now?"

"I've never been more sure in my life," I said, lifting my chin, his mouth crashing into mine again as we fell back onto the bed together.

CHAPTER 31

OLFE

IT WAS as if my entire life had led up to this moment.

December lay before me, as beautiful as if a star had fallen from the sky and fallen naked into the bed, shimmering and sparkling like a diamond that was custom made just for me.

I'd spent so many nights imagining this. The fantasy version of her body warming me through the coldest, loneliest nights of my life. The beauty I'd imagined I'd find once her clothes were peeled off was nothing compared to the stunning reality lying in front of me.

"You're...you're...just stunning," I whispered, as I drank in the vision of her. I almost felt like I must be dreaming again. *Could this be real? After all this time?*

I reached down after pulling off my clothes, my palm sliding along the outside of her thigh, just to prove to myself that this was really happening. Her skin was soft as silk, smooth and tan, quivering under my touch.

She stared up at me with awe in her eyes that left me humbled. Could she really have loved me as much as I loved her all this time?

I'd always wondered what things would be like if we reconnected. I'd wondered if things would be the same, if we'd still be as close, after all the years had put so much distance between us. We weren't the same people, not even close.

We'd grown up. Changed.

So very much.

But after spending this time with her, after kissing her, and looking down at her, open and welcoming me with her spread limbs, I knew that our love for each other had only grown stronger over the years, despite the distance.

I moved towards her, my body on fire for the one person I'd spent my life yearning for.

My mouth found hers as she wrapped herself around me, her thighs sliding around my hips, her arms pulling me in close as her mouth opened, accepting mine as her hips pushed up towards me, our bodies begging for the connection we'd always needed.

CHAPTER 32

ECEMBER

THE FAINT GLOW of the moon was the only light in the room, but it provided just enough for me to drink in Wolfe's hulking frame, his body etched with scrawling tattoos, his dark eyes thirsty with lust.

He kissed me passionately, the pent-up emotion flowing between us like a dam had been broken, finally allowing the love to pour out between us.

His hardness nudged against my center, a promise of all the primal pleasure I'd been missing out on all my life. I raised my hips, wanting him, needing him, my body begging for him.

He tore his mouth from mine, staring deeply into my eyes as he slowly slid inside of me. I whimpered, my heart filling with so much emotion I thought it might burst. Slowly, inch by delicious inch, he thrust inside me smoothly, my thighs tightening around him as I pulled him deeper.

He paused, looking down at me with wonder.

"December," he growled, my name falling thickly from his lips.

"I know," I whispered, my eyes shining with love-filled tears. He pulled out slightly, sliding back in, the feeling exquisitely gratifying. "Again, please, again…"

"Oh, babe," he moaned, his hips rocking back and forth as he filled me with his hardness over and over.

"Wolfe," I whispered his name, like a promise on the tip of my tongue that I'd yearned to fulfill. "Wolfe, Wolfe, yes, please…"

He rocked against me, filling me up, my hands sliding over his skin, the heat between us building as he picked up the pace, our bodies starving for each other.

He groaned and growled, his mouth crashing into mine again as he worked his cock in and out of me, my body quivering with pleasure under his decadent assault.

I'd dreamed of him above me like this for years, late at night when I was all alone, when I dared to allow myself the secret pleasure of thinking about him, my fingers finding the release I needed so badly, as my lips caressed his name in the darkness.

But it was never as good as this.

The real thing.

The real man, kind and loving and beautiful and sensual, his body merging with mine like two parts of a puzzle fitting together with perfect precision.

He pushed into me harder with each thrust, pressing deeper and deeper until I was crying out in pleasure, his cock slamming into me, pulling every ounce of pleasure in my body to the surface until I crashed over the edge of bliss, shaking and crying and shuddering as I clung to him like his body was the essence of life.

When he exploded inside of me, a white-hot heat that ripped through his body violently, his mouth firmly planted against mine, his tongue delving deep as possible as he roared into it, I welcomed his fiery offering, widening my thighs, and welcoming him home at last.

CHAPTER 33

OLFE

Waking up with December in my arms, our bare skin sliding together, left my heart swollen with love. She stirred, the morning sunlight in her hair, as she snuggled up against my chest. I pulled her close, wishing with every part of my soul that we'd get to wake up like this for the rest of our lives.

We'd wasted too much time, too much life, too much love.

The dueling emotions inside of me — love and rage — were separate beings that fought for consciousness. I fantasized about the revenge I was going to unleash on Shane in the same moments that I fantasized about my future with December.

It was a mind fuck, but I was all in.

No matter what happened today, nothing could take away the night I'd spent with her.

I didn't want to wake her. I knew she was tormented with worry for Leo and she seemed so peaceful sleeping, her head resting against my chest, her breath rising and falling so effortlessly.

It killed me to see her cry. To see the fear in her eyes.

If we could get through this, with Leo safely on the other side, I knew nothing would ever come between us again.

Whatever ended up happening with Shane, I would never let him back in our lives.

If he lived.

I still wasn't sure I was going to let that happen, and the anger boiling inside of me had other ideas.

Outside of a few fights in the pen, I'd never really been a violent guy. Even when I was, it was for work or self-defense.

But the murderous, vengeful fantasies forming in my head told a different story about who I was, leaving me questioning myself.

I finally chalked it up to the fact that I was doing what I'd always done — protecting December to the best of my ability. Now, Leo was a part of that, too. As he should be.

I wondered what he was like now. I'd only met him once, when he was very young. Now, he was a young man, no doubt with his own thoughts and ideals of what his own family and future should look like. I couldn't help but wonder if he'd accept me into it.

I hoped like hell he would, though.

We could work out all the logistics later, but I knew there was no way in hell I'd walk away again.

I pulled December closer, inhaling the sweet perfume of her soft hair against my chin. I looked out the window and saw that it was snowing again, soft billowing flakes falling gently through the air.

And yet, I was warmer than I'd ever been with December in my arms.

December, the snow, the feel of her body next to mine, the love flowing between us — I wanted it all to last forever.

CHAPTER 34

*D*ECEMBER

ASTORIA WAS BEAUTIFUL, but I didn't really register any of that beauty. With Wolfe holding my hand firmly, we walked into the convenience store on the marina.

A bell rang out over our heads as the door closed behind us, warmth enveloping us as we walked in.

The man behind the counter had kind eyes and I walked straight over to him with a smile.

"Hello," he said, his voice as warm and kind as his eyes.

"Hi," I said, pulling my phone out of my pocket. "The other day, someone from this store called the cops about a man and a young boy that they were concerned about."

"Oh, yes, that was me," he nodded.

"My son is missing," I said, my voice shaking every time I said those painful words. "I was wondering if you could take a look at this photo and tell me if he's the boy you saw."

I pulled up a picture of Leo, smiling with joy next to Lucy and fought back the tears that threatened to spill out. I gave the man my phone and he stared down at the photo.

"Oh, look at that smile," he said. "I am pretty sure that's him. Although, unfortunately, he wasn't smiling and he looked quite upset. I was pretty sure that he was trying to signal to me that something was wrong but the man he was with came in before I could get any information out of him."

I nodded, breathless. I pulled up an old picture of Shane and showed him that.

"Is that the man?"

"Yes!" The man said, his eyes lighting up. "That's definitely them."

"Thank you!" I said. "And you said they went north after leaving here?"

"That's right," he said. "Oh! I pulled up a video from my surveillance. I kept thinking the cops might want it, but nobody has come by to get it yet."

"Can we see it?" Wolfe asked. He'd been silent behind me this whole time, quietly letting me talk to the man.

"Sure!" he said, coming out from around the corner. "Come back into my office."

We followed him into a tiny, dingy office behind the coolers and he pulled the video up on his computer. In seconds, Leo appeared on the screen.

I gasped in joy. My boy! He was alive. He was okay!

"That's him, right?" the man asked.

"It is," I said. I'd have known his face and his walk anywhere, despite the blurry footage. We watched as he stood in front of the counter for a minute as he unloaded a bunch of snacks on the counter and stood in front of the man. I could see his eye was slightly swollen and dark and it broke my heart to think he was hurting. But at least he was alive.

Seconds later, Shane walked in, his face angry and pinched.

After paying, they walked out and disappeared from view.

"Thank you so much," I said to the man.

"We should get going," Wolfe said. "They can't be too far away."

"Good luck, miss. I hope you find your boy."

"We'll find him," Wolfe said, with a determined nod. "You did the right thing by calling the cops."

"Well, I thought so, too. They said they'd call the Coast Guard, but I don't know what happened with that."

"We appreciate your help," I said.

Wolfe and I walked back to the boat and joined the others.

"Well?" Slade asked.

"It was definitely them. Let's get moving."

"Excellent," Slade said, snow falling around him as he stood on the deck. "We're getting so close! Gonna be a great day!"

"A great day?" I asked.

"Well, yeah, like I said before —."

"—any day is a great day to kick some ass," Wolfe finished.

"There ya go, brother!" Slade laughed in agreement.

Storm started up the boat and we pulled away from the dock, lurching Slade unexpectedly to the floor of the deck.

We all laughed as Wreck helped him back up to his feet.

"Man, these fucking boots were not made for this slick shit," he said, without the slightest twinge of embarrassment. "I don't think I'm made for it, either."

"Looks like we found your Achilles heel," Wolfe said.

"No fucking way, dude," Slade said, shaking his head. "I'm invincible!"

He made a move to go towards the stairs leading to the cabin, but slipped again, falling flat on his ass all over again.

We all roared with laughter and I felt the pain in my heart subside just a little.

CHAPTER 35

OLFE

"HEY, brother, I was listening to the scanners again, for the Coast Guard," Riot said. He'd called again a few hours after we left Astoria and I'd walked away from the others to talk to him.

"And?" I asked, bracing myself for bad news.

"Sounds like they lost contact with one of their boats, just a little bit north of where y'all are right now. No mention of Shane or the boy, but it seems a little fishy. It may not be related at all. I just wanted to mention it. They're sending a search crew out now."

"Okay," I replied, absorbing the information. Riot was right, it could mean anything. "And Shane's GPS is still turned off?"

"I haven't had any more hits on it."

"Right."

"How's December holding up?"

"She's strong as an ox. She's amazing, actually."

"Sounds like you have a lot of respect for her."

"It's a lot more than that, brother."

"Love?"

I laughed. "What's stronger than love? Whatever it is, that's it."

"Damn, okay," he laughed, before turning serious. "Listen, Wolfe, I wanted to talk to you about something else."

"What's up?"

"Well, you know me. I like to dig, right?"

"Sure," I agreed.

"Well, I hope you don't mind, but while I was researching Shane to try to find any clues about where he might be going, I pulled up a lot of extra stuff, too."

"What did you find out?"

"Well, I looked through all of his emails, going back several years. And I found something that seemed a little weird."

"What?"

"He was researching your case a few years ago. It was while you were still locked up. First, I just saw some information requests — like, he was requesting all the police reports from the shooting at the convenience store. But then, he started requesting forensic reports, too. Ballistic shit."

"Ballistics?"

"It was weird, man. And I don't want to overstep or bring up bad memories for you."

"It was a long time ago, man. I'm fine. Don't worry about me."

"Okay, well I started looking at the reports myself. And I found some discrepancies that were really odd."

"Go on," I said, my curiosity piqued.

"Okay, so both the clerk and Leo were killed, right?"

"Yes."

"And there was no surveillance, so all the investigators had to go on was forensic stuff, which was just bullet casings and shit like that."

"Right."

"Well, something doesn't add up. Not with the story you told me when you first joined up with the Gods."

"Like what?"

"Well, you said that Leo and Shane went in to rob the place. And you said that the clerk shot Leo and Shane shot the clerk with his own gun, right?"

"Yeah."

"Well, the thing is, man — the bullets shouldn't match. But they do."

"What?" I asked, confused.

"The same gun that shot the clerk is the same gun that shot Leo."

It was like time stopped in that moment. I'd spent years staring up at the ceiling wondering how it had all gone down. When Shane got back in the car that night, he specifically said, "He shot him." It only made sense that he meant the clerk shot Leo. I just assumed that Shane shot the clerk after that.

"And well, brother, the clerk did have a gun. It was found right next to his body, on the floor behind the counter."

"I saw it," I said.

"Yeah, but that gun was never fired. And the gun that shot them both was never recovered. Just the bullet casings were left behind."

The rage that had been living inside of me was rattling like a beast in a cage. The only thing this could mean is that Shane shot Leo, and the clerk, too. I'd never thought he would have shot his friend, my friend.

"Why didn't any of this come out before?"

"Probably because you confessed, man. Cops and investigators are fucking lazy. Once you confessed, nobody fucking cared about paying any attention to the facts. I took a look at your confession, too. I know it was a long time ago, but it said you told the cops that showed up that the clerk shot Leo, so you shot the clerk, right?"

"Yeah, that's right."

"So, as far as they were concerned, it was an open and shut case. Hell, they never even did an autopsy on either of the bodies, if you can fucking believe that. That's some lazy ass police work."

"Yeah, well, Lincoln County isn't exactly known for their superior skills."

"I guess you're right there."

My head spinning, I tried to reconcile this new information with what I'd believed for over a decade. I was reeling, my body pouring sweat as I stood on the deck, soft snow cascading onto my shoulders.

"I'm so sorry, man. I know this is a lot to take in," Riot said.

"It is," I said. "But I'm grateful you looked into it. The truth is always best."

"What are you going to do?"

I paused, his question catching me off guard. It didn't take but a second to reply, though, because I knew now, more than ever, what I needed to do.

"I'm going to fucking kill him."

CHAPTER 36

ECEMBER

WHEN WOLFE CAME BACK from talking to Riot, something had changed in him.

"Everything okay?" I asked, feeling the tension rolling off his body.

"Yeah," he said, his voice gruff. "Riot heard on the scanner that the Coast Guard lost touch with one of their officers. Not sure if it's related, he just wanted to let me know."

"Oh."

He turned away, avoiding my eyes. I couldn't help but wonder if there was something he wasn't telling me, but I didn't want to push. Since waking up in his arms this morning, my body was still tingling from his delicious touch and I had never felt more connected to him.

I'd never felt more alive.

He brushed a kiss across my forehead and pulled away.

"I need to go talk with the guys," he said, heading up to the deck and leaving me alone in the cabin.

I needed to stay busy — with my body on fire from his touch, and my heart full of worry for Leo, I was a hot mess of emotion. To combat the urge to break down completely, I started making lunch. I filled a huge platter with several different kinds of sandwiches, before going up to get the guys, who were so deep in conversation, they didn't notice my presence.

"You sure about that, man?" Slade asked Wolfe.

"I'm sure," he nodded.

"Well, you know we'll have your back, before and after," Wreck said.

"I appreciate that," Wolfe said.

My curiosity got the best of me and I couldn't help but pipe in.

"Sure of what?" I asked.

They turned to me in surprise, and Wolfe gave them all a glance. They shut their mouths quickly and turned to him, waiting for him to explain.

Wolfe came over and wrapped his arms around me, leaning down to whisper in my ear. "I'm sure that I love you, babe."

I squinted up at him, knowing full well they weren't talking about that.

"Right," I nodded, my tone laced with obvious skepticism. "I made lunch. Sandwiches."

"Oh, shit yeah," Slade said, jumping up and gingerly walking past us so he wouldn't slip again. Wreck followed him, leaving us alone.

"Thanks, babe," Wolfe said, kissing me quickly before going down with them, avoiding any chance for me to question him further. I shook it off, figuring whatever was going on, he'd tell me eventually. I trusted him not to keep something important from me.

I walked into the wheelhouse and joined Storm there.

"Hey," I greeted him with a smile.

"Hi, December." Storm was warm and kind, just like the others, but he was much quieter.

"I made lunch. Want me to bring you a few sandwiches?"

"Sure," he shrugged. "That'd be great. How are you holding up?"

"I'm okay," I replied. "I just want my boy back. Do you think we're getting close?"

"I really do. We've made great time, and are probably right on their tail."

"How will we know when we're close?" I asked.

"When we see Shane's boat. I've been on the lookout."

"Right," I said, feeling disappointed. "Are we just looking for a needle in a haystack here?"

"If it were summer, then it might be a lot harder. But most people stay off the water this time of year, so the traffic is light. I'm actually very confident we're going to find them, most likely by the end of the day."

"I'm so glad you think so," I said. "I'll go get those sandwiches and be right back."

"Chin up, December. You'll have your boy back soon," he winked at me and flashed me a crooked grin, his hopefulness a sliver of light piercing my dark, worried heart.

CHAPTER 37

OLFE

"Everybody on deck!"

Storm's call jolted us all to attention. We'd been hanging out in the cabin watching a movie, but at his words, we all scrambled to our feet and ran upstairs.

"What's going on?" I asked, my heart racing in my chest. I'd been struggling to contain the fury I was feeling since I'd talked to Riot. I hated doing it, but I kept the information he'd given me from December until I could process my feelings.

But all I really felt was pure, burning rage and the only way I could think of processing anything was burning Shane alive with it. December had enough to think about right now and the knowledge that her son's father had killed her twin brother was not something I felt like she needed to take on. She was strong, she could handle it, but why put her through that kind of suffering?

I kept my mouth shut and did my best to stay calm.

Inside, a storm was brewing, though. I was itching to get my hands on Shane and I knew Storm wouldn't call us up here for nothing.

"Look!" He pointed at a boat in the distance. With its all-round light visible, it was obvious they'd anchored in place for the night. "It's them."

Storm handed me his binoculars and I peered out at the boat.

"It's definitely them, the numbers match the title and registration."

"Sure do," I said, nodding. My palms started sweating and my heart began pounding in my chest, as a rush of adrenaline pulsed through my veins.

"Oh, my god," December said. "Can we get closer? How do I get on his boat?"

"You don't," I growled, a surge of protection mixing with all my other emotions.

"What?" she asked, looking at me defiantly.

"I'm going to handle this," I said.

"I need to get to Leo!"

"And I need to get to Shane first," I said. "I'm not going to let him near you, December."

"But —."

"But nothing!" I said, looking down at her gently. "Shane's unpredictable. I'm not allowing you to put yourself in a dangerous situation. Do you trust me?"

She looked up at me in tears, slowly nodding. "Yes."

"Good." I kissed her firmly, before turning to Storm. "How close can we get?"

"Pretty close," he said. "I don't see anyone on deck and I don't think they've spotted us yet. I'm turning off our lights and we'll inch a bit closer."

"I can swim over," I said.

"It's fucking freezing, dude," Slade said.

"I don't care," I replied.

"Wait!" Wreck said. "I spotted a few wet suits in the closet. Maybe one will fit."

"I'll make it fit."

I walked downstairs as Wolfe turned the lights off and slowed our boat to a crawl. The wet suit looked impossibly small, but I went into December's bedroom and stripped, forcing my limbs into it. Once I had it on, I took a minute to look around.

December's clothes were piled in a corner and the covers were still tangled up from our night in her bed, and I knew that it would be a long while before we got to enjoy a night like that again.

Even if everything went well, she would need to attend to her son. He would surely be traumatized from his father's actions and she might not have time for me for weeks. I closed my eyes, flashing through the night in my head to engrave it into my memory one last time before I went to face my enemy.

CHAPTER 38

ECEMBER

OF COURSE, I trusted him.

That didn't mean I didn't want to get to my son as fast as possible.

It killed me watching him jump in the water once we were much closer to Shane's boat. I held my breath as he swam over quickly, his strong limbs maneuvering easily in the water.

I felt like my heart was going to burst from my chest. Slade, standing next to me, threw an arm around me and pulled me close. I leaned into him, thankful for his support and warmth.

"I'm terrified," I whispered.

"Don't be," Slade said. "Your man there is fearless. He's strong. Smart. And he's got a waterproof backpack full of firearms and ammunition, if he needs it. Shane's the one that should be terrified."

I took a deep breath, unable to reply as we watched Wolfe approach the boat and pull himself aboard. He crouched down, waiting for a moment before opening his backpack and pulling out a gun.

Fear gripped me, despite Slade's reassurances.

It was then that I realized just how much I truly loved Wolfe.

If anything happened to him, or Leo, I knew I'd never be able to go on.

They were everything to me and I just needed them both safe.

CHAPTER 39

OLFE

SILENCE BLANKETED THE BOAT, the darkness lending a stillness to the night like some delicate veil I tried not to pierce.

I wanted to surprise Shane. I needed to have the upper hand.

But first, I needed to make sure Leo was safe.

I crept forward, doing my best not to make a sound. The lights were on in the cabin and I looked through the little window leading down to it.

Shane sat on a small couch, watching television with a bottle of Patron on a small nearby table and a shot glass in his hand. My eyes scanned over the rest of the cabin, looking for Leo.

He was nowhere in sight.

I inched down to the stern, hoping he might be on deck and I could get him off the boat quickly. In the distance, I could see our boat inching closer towards us in the dark.

Leo wasn't on deck anywhere, though.

I looked in the window again, waiting for him to appear. It was possible he was in the bathroom or a corner, but I could see the bed was empty and no other movement seemed to be happening.

Shane laughed at the television, breaking the silence.

Worried by Leo's absence, I decided I had no other choice but to confront Shane head on.

With my finger on the trigger of my gun, I started down the stairs.

CHAPTER 40

 HANE

I DIDN'T EVEN HEAR him coming.

"Hello, Shane."

It was his voice that alerted me to him when he was inches away and I jumped to my feet in surprise.

"You!" I shouted. I'd have known those eyes anywhere, even though he looked like a completely different person than when I'd last seen him. "What the fuck are you doing here?"

I looked behind him, completely confused. He seemed to be alone. I'd have heard, or even felt it, if another boat approached. So, how the hell was he on my boat now?

"I came to see you," Wolfe said, his voice a deep growl.

He was monstrously huge. Jacked up like fucking Schwarzenegger. I guess prison will do that to anyone.

"In the middle of nowhere in the fucking ocean?" I asked.

"Where's the boy?" he demanded.

"The boy? Leo? You mean my son?"

"Where is he?"

"Oh, I get it," I laughed. "Of course, she'd send you. That fucking bitch!"

He moved closer, getting in my face.

"Where is the boy?" he asked, repeating himself.

I laughed again, shaking my head.

"You're way too late, asshole."

CHAPTER 41

OLFE

I DIDN'T BELIEVE HIM. I couldn't.

If Leo was gone, then I'd lose December, too.

I took a step forward, closing the distance between us.

"I had high hopes for you, Shane," I began. "I thought maybe, after the shooting, you'd do the right thing. Be a fucking man. But you were never capable of that in the first place, were you? You're nothing but a spineless piece of shit. You always have been."

"Fuck you," he said. "You're a fucking idiot."

"I used to be," I agreed. "That night, when I thought you had it in you to grow up. To treat December and Leo like they deserved. If I had known what a prick you'd end up being, I would have let you take the fall."

"I never asked you for anything!"

"No, you didn't. And that's on me. For giving you the benefit of the doubt. But the rest of the shit — that's all on you, Shane. I know what you did."

He looked up at me in surprise and I saw the truth right there in his eyes.

"That's right, you murderous bastard. That night, when you got in the car, you said the clerk shot Leo. But it wasn't true, was it? You're the one who shot Leo."

"You don't fucking know that!"

"I do," I nodded. "The ballistics reports told the truth. You got so lucky, didn't you? I was a chump for taking the fall. I never should have. I should have let the cops fucking have you that night. But December had just told me she was pregnant. I did it for her."

"Oh, like there was ever any doubt about that! You were in love with her!"

"You're right about that. I was. I still am, in fact. And before I kill you, Shane, you need to know that she's mine now. You'll never get near her again. You'll never lay eyes on her again, let alone a hand."

"You won't kill me," he said, lifting his chin. "You don't have it in you. And fucking Leo deserved it, goddammit!"

"No, he didn't," I said. "Leo was a good man."

"We were fucking kids, Wolfe! Look, it was Leo's idea to steal the beer. I had a gun in my pocket, but he didn't even know that. When the clerk pulled out his gun when we tried to run out with the beer, I shot him to protect Leo."

"Cut the bullshit!" I shouted, my anger rising like a flame to the surface.

"It's true!" He insisted. "But Leo freaked out, man! He said he was going to tell the cops I did it. He was a fucking pussy."

"And so you shot him, too."

"I had to kill Leo! To shut him up! I had just saved his life and he was going to rat me out?" He cried, his eyes wild. "There was no fucking way I'd survive in prison."

"That's true, they would have eaten your weak ass alive."

"Look, man, I'm grateful for you. I never said that, did I? You didn't have to do that, though. I would have gotten off, no matter what. But you had to be the big man. You had to step up and protect a woman that didn't even belong to you. How fucking stupid was that? To confess to a killing you didn't commit? Who does that?"

I pulled out my gun, aiming it straight at his ugly, murderous face.

"Oh!" he said, taking a step back with a laugh. "Does this mean you enjoyed prison? You want to go back? For life this time?"

"I'm never going back," I growled, cocking the hammer.

CHAPTER 42

EO

I'D BEEN TRYING to pick the lock on the door for an hour straight. I had a toothpick and it was almost shredded when I heard the lock finally click open.

Dad had locked us in the bathroom after he shot the guy on the Coast Guard boat and I was desperately trying to get out. I was terrified, and Lucy could tell. She'd been leaning into my legs and staring up at me with her big black eyes. When the lock finally opened, she began dancing around my legs.

"Shhh," I said, gingerly cracking the door and peeking out.

I'd heard voices but I wasn't sure who it was. Now, I saw a large man in a wet suit standing in front of Dad, his back to me. My eyes widened as I listened.

"I had to kill Leo! To shut him up! I had just saved his life and he was going to rat me out?" Dad shouted. "There was no fucking way I'd survive in prison."

My head spun at his words. Dad was the one who killed Uncle

Leo? How could he have let someone else go to prison for something he'd done? I'd known my Dad was an awful person, but the full impact of just how horrible he was hit me so hard I couldn't breathe.

If he could kill one of his best friends, he could definitely kill me, too.

Neither of them noticed me as I snuck out of the bathroom, gently closing the door and leaving Lucy inside.

Dad's gun was on a table by the stairs.

I crawled over to it, pulling it down and crawling back behind the kitchen counter to hide and listen.

"That's true, they would have eaten your weak ass alive," the man said.

"Look, man, I'm grateful for you. You didn't have to do that, though. I would have gotten off, no matter what. But you had to be the big man. You had to step up and protect a woman that didn't even belong to you. How fucking stupid was that? To confess to a killing you didn't commit? Who does that? Oh!" Dad said, laughing. "Does this mean you enjoyed prison? You want to go back? For life this time?"

"I'm never going back," the man said, the sound of a hammer cocking echoing through the cabin.

Fear ripped through me, my hands shaking as I checked to make sure there were bullets in Dad's gun.

CHAPTER 43

OLFE

"I'm going to ask you one more time, Shane. Where's Leo?"

He scoffed, his arrogance on full display. Pulsing with rage, my finger was itching to pull the trigger.

"I told you," he said. "He's fucking gone. December's going to be fucking crushed. So, enjoy your new broken bitch, you goddamn idiot. Maybe I'll kill her next, just to fuck with you."

"Fine," I said, pressing the gun to his forehead. "You just signed your death warrant, motherfucker."

"Oh? You liked prison that much, huh? You shoot me and you'll go to prison for life. I'm a fucking cop, dumbass! You'll never be free again, Wolfe."

His words didn't faze me.

The thought of a life in prison didn't faze me.

If he'd really killed Leo, and managed to kill December's son, too, then I'd happily go to prison if necessary

But the Gods had my back. I knew we'd clean up this mess and there was no way in hell I'd get busted for it.

Pulling the trigger was going to be the best thing I'd ever done in my life.

"Killing your sorry ass will make it all worth it," I growled.

CHAPTER 44

ECEMBER

THE CLOSER AND closer we got to the boat, the more I thought I was going to just fall apart completely. My entire body was shivering, not from the biting cold, but from fear.

We were just a few feet away when a gunshot rang out, breaking through the silence in a violent explosion of sound.

I jumped into Slade's arms, my eyes wide, my body trembling.

"It's okay, baby girl," he said. He looked over at Storm and Wreck. "I'm jumping on."

He pulled away from me and started to climb over the edge of our boat and jumped onto Shane's stern. Without thinking, I followed him, ignoring Wreck calling my name as I climbed over the edge. All I could think about was Leo. I had to get to him.

"Stay back!" Slade hissed, staying in front of me as we snuck towards the cabin. He pulled a handgun out of his boot, pointing it in front of him as we headed down the stairs.

The scene in front of me left my blood cold.

Shane lay on the floor, a river of blood pouring out of his head. I whipped my head around and saw Wolfe taking a gun out of Leo's hands.

"Leo!" I cried. He spotted me and ran towards me, his arms wrapping around me tightly.

"Mom!" He sobbed so hard I could hardly understand his words. "I shot Dad! He killed the man on the boat! He killed Uncle Leo! He was going to kill me and Lucy, too!"

"Shh, baby, you're okay now, you're okay," I said. He was shaking with fear and I held him as close as I could, my eyes wild, trying to make sense of it all.

Wolfe stood staring down at Shane's motionless body, the gun he'd taken from Leo still in his hand. Slade rushed over to him, taking the gun from him gently.

"You good, dude?" Slade asked, looking him up and down. "You get hit?"

He shook his head, slowly, "No, man. I'm alright."

Slade put the gun down and walked over to Shane, kneeling down and checking his pulse.

"Is he dead?" Wolfe asked, as Wreck and Storm ran into the cabin with us.

"Sure the fuck is," he replied, standing back up.

Wolfe nodded, slowly turning his head to look over at me and Leo.

He walked over, putting his arms around us and holding us tightly.

"It's over," he growled, as we sobbed in his arms. "Nobody is ever going to hurt either of you again."

EPILOGUE

 HRISTMAS EVE

"MOM, LOOK AT HIM!" Leo shouted, his eyes lit up with joy as Oliver landed gracefully on his shoulder. Lucy rested at his feet peacefully, ignoring the owls all together.

"Wow," December said, beaming at her son. Since they'd arrived at the Gods' clubhouse a few days ago, Leo had bonded with the two owls that seemed to always be hanging around. "I think he likes you!"

Olivia sat on the porch railing, quietly watching with her wise, blinking eyes as her partner snuggled his beak against the boy's cheek. Never one to be left out, she took flight, landing on December's thigh as she sat on the swing.

"I think they like both of you," Wolfe said, smiling as December reached down to pet her soft feathers. He sat next to December as closely as possible, having not left her side for more than a few minutes since they'd made it safely back to shore.

The road ahead would be a long one for them, full of pain and grief, but they were determined to brave it together. The Gods had done what they always did — they took care of everything and wrapped up all the loose ends. As far as anyone was concerned, Shane brought Leo back to December and then quit his job and took off on his own for a years-long adventure on his boat.

Nobody would be looking for him for quite some time, if ever.

They were finally free.

Colorful, blinking lights lit up the tall swaying trees surrounding the clubhouse, a soft dusting of snow perched on their branches. The Gods had welcomed December and Leo with wide-open arms and for the last few days, they'd relished in the peace and love that blanketed them during their stay.

Soon, Leo would have to go back to school and they'd both have to move on with their life, as best as they could, but this time, with the support of a loving man, and their newly acquired family of Gods.

But for now, it was still December and the magic of Christmas was in the air.

"I love it here, Mom, can't we stay longer?" Leo asked.

"We already talked about that, Leo," December replied. "You have to go to school and therapy. It's best if we stay where we are, at least until the school year is over."

"And then can we live here?" he asked, his eyes brightly shining with hope. He'd taken to Wolfe right away, and didn't mind at all that his Mom liked him so much. He thought it was great that she was so happy now.

December laughed, looking over at Wolfe.

"We'll work it out," Wolfe said, his low gruff voice a profound source of comfort. His confidence and courage was contagious and December lifted her chin, knowing that whatever happened from here on out, that they would indeed work it out — together.

Olivia and Oliver flew away, landing on the branch of a nearby Douglas fir, the lights illuminating their feathers with bright shades of red and green.

Wolfe reached over and pulled December closer, his arm wrapped around her shoulders. She looked up at him and he brushed a soft kiss across her lips. She sighed and leaned into his warmth.

"I never imagined I'd be hoping for the dark days of December to never end," she softly laughed.

"As far as I'm concerned," Wolfe replied, "I'd be just fine with December lasting forever."

"Unfortunately, it can't be December forever. To be honest, I'm ready for a fresh start. A new life," she paused, her eyes peering deeply into his. "I'm excited to start a new life with you, Wolfe."

He reached down, cupping her cheek with his warm palm, staring down into the eyes of the only love he'd ever known.

"Forever?" he asked, a slow smile stretching across his face.

"Forever," she whispered, kissing him gently, the life she'd never thought possible stretching out before her like a long-lost promise finally delivered.

THE END

ABOUT THE AUTHOR

Honey Palomino lives in the Pacific Northwest with her husband and two hilarious dogs.

She's best known for her Gods of Chaos Motorcycle Club Series, which follows a group of golden-hearted bikers on their journey to help people get out of troubling situations when they can't turn to traditional resources for help.

Most days, she can be found sitting under the towering pines in her backyard and dreaming of twisty new plots to entice her readers with.

THANK YOU SO MUCH FOR READING
THE GODS OF CHAOS MOTORCYCLE CLUB SERIES!
THE GODS OF CHAOS MOTORCYCLE CLUB IS AN ONGOING SERIES.
WE HOPE YOU'LL CONTINUE READING!

If you're interested in checking out the rest of Honey Palomino's work, including all of the Gods of Chaos MC installments, you can do so at:
www.amazon.com/Honey-Palomino/e/B00DR2B2J6

Sign up to receive news about new releases:
goo.gl/forms/LiStOjAsPro8Ycx73
Find Honey on facebook:
www.facebook.com/HoneyPalomino1/
Find Honey on Instagram:
www.instagram.com/honeypalomino/
Follow Honey on twitter:
www.twitter.com/honeypalomino
Email Honey at:
honeypalomino@gmail.com